ROAD TO SOMEWHERE

BOOK TWO IN THE CLEARWATER SERIES

JULIE MAYERSON BROWN

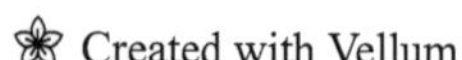
Created with Vellum

For my Guys
Mark, Mickey, Sammy

1

Patty Sullivan sat at her kitchen table eating Lucky Charms from the box and scrolling through Instagram.

A low whine, like an off-key hum, groaned above her, and a thin crack zigzagged across the ceiling as if drawn by an invisible hand.

She stood, frowned, and angled her head.

The crack widened, and her ceiling split like a raw egg. Chunks of plaster and wood fell onto the table.

"Holy shit!"

A pipe burst, and a deluge of cold water soaked her from head to toe.

Patty jumped back, gasping and choking, but before she could catch her breath, the hole above her head expanded, and a white porcelain bathtub crashed through. It squashed the chair where she'd been sitting.

A brush with death was not a good way to start the day.

Patty stood on the lawn and watched the firefighters wrap yellow caution tape around her Venice Beach duplex. She clutched her head, tufts of red hair sticking out between her fingers.

"Miss?"

"Huh?" She pivoted at the sound of a deep voice.

"I'm Captain Brandt. What's your name?" He wore a blue uniform and heavy black boots. He was bald with thick forearms covered with curly gray hair.

"Patty Sullivan." Her lower lip trembled, and her vision blurred with tears.

The man towered over her. He straightened his wire-framed glasses. "Do you mind if I ask how old you are?"

"I'm twenty-nine."

The captain's eyebrows shot up. "You are?"

She dragged her sleeve under her nose and sniffled. At just over five feet tall and wearing a faded Minnie Mouse nightshirt, she understood his surprise. "I know I don't look it, but I am."

"Okay, sorry." He gave her an apologetic smile. "It's rude to ask a woman her age, but I had to."

"It's okay," she said.

The man was growing on her.

"Does anybody live in the second-floor apartment?"

She shook her head. "It's been empty for at least a month."

"Hmm, that could've been the problem." Captain Brandt put his hands on his hips. "Probably a leak nobody noticed. These old houses converted into apartments have all kinds of structural issues. That bathroom probably wasn't even to code."

Patty didn't care about structure or codes. She shivered. It was a cool morning in May, and the breeze blew through her wet shirt. "Can I go inside and change?"

"Yeah. But just so you know, we're gonna have to red-tag the place."

"What does that mean?" She pushed on the corner of her left eye, willing it not to twitch.

"Means you can't stay here."

Sharp blades of grass poked her bare feet. "For how long?"

"Hard to say." The weathered-looking captain scratched the top of his head. "Go on in to change and grab what you need. I'll give you fifteen minutes."

"Fifteen minutes?" Disbelief gave way to panic. She wasn't so fond of him anymore. "I can't pack that fast!"

"Twenty then. And be sure to take your valuables. Condemned places attract thieves."

Condemned?

Patty scurried inside, her teeth chattering and body trembling. She peered into the kitchen. Other than the hole in the ceiling, the flooded floor, and the bathtub, it wasn't that bad. Living with no kitchen was doable—she hardly used it anyway.

The clock on the stove ticked, reminding her that time was short. She bolted into the bathroom and turned on the shower. A few drops of water dribbled from the spout.

Something, or someone, tapped on the window beside the sink.

Patty pulled up the shade to see Captain Brandt's face on the other side of the glass. She opened the window an inch.

"Just so you know, we had to shut the water off. You can use the toilet, but it ain't gonna, you know, flush."

Well, that was awkward. "Gotcha."

Annoyed to have lost a minute, she went to her room and threw on the jeans and sweatshirt she'd worn the night before.

Patty took a tremulous breath. She had only minutes to pack up her life. If the place were on fire, what would she grab?

Not much, because there *wasn't* much. In three years, she'd moved four times, shedding belongings with every relocation.

At the top of the short list of items Patty valued was her father's silver money clip. He'd given it to her the day she'd left for college. When she was little, her dad had let her hold the money clip every Sunday during church. She'd polished it with the hem of her dress throughout the long service, making the surface shiny and smooth.

She found it in her sock drawer and tucked it into her backpack.

Her tiny closet was jammed with clothes she should've discarded ages ago. Without a thought as to what she'd need or want, she yanked pants and skirts and shirts off hangers and threw them onto the bed.

Someone poked her shoulder.

"Oh!" She jumped. "You scared me."

Captain Brandt stood behind her. Apparently, destruction to one's home voided all rules of etiquette.

"Sorry I startled you, but you need to get a move on."

"I need more time."

The captain shook his head. "No can do."

Patty sat on top of her clothes and pouted. "What if I refuse to go?"

"I'd probably have you arrested."

"Then at least I'd have a place to sleep." She tried to swallow her tears, but they were impossible to contain.

"Oh, no," Captain Brandt said. "Please don't cry. Where's your suitcase?"

That made her cry even harder. "It broke. I threw it away." She fell face down onto her pillow.

"Calm down. There's a box of Hefty bags in the truck. I'll be right back."

"Thank you," she said, her voice muffled against the pillow.

Patty lifted her head and wiped her face on the sheet, breathing in the faint scent of laundry detergent.

By the time he returned, she'd pulled herself together.

"Sorry I cried in front of you."

"I understand." He handed her two black trash bags. "Now please, pack up quickly."

With no time for picking and choosing, Patty stuffed as much as she could into the bags. She went back to the bathroom and swept everything off the counter into her oversized purse.

A young fireman in yellow pants and suspenders knocked on the doorjamb. "Captain sent me in to see if you, uh, if you need any help."

"He sent you in to hurry me up, didn't he?"

"Well, kinda. Want me to take those bags to your car?"

"Yes, please."

He lifted one in each hand and carried them out.

Patty surveyed the apartment and her random assortment of stuff. If someone broke in and stole everything, she wouldn't even care. Except for the cozy purple throw blanket her best friend, Cece, had given her for her birthday. She grabbed it off the arm of the couch and left without even locking the door.

The fireman stood beside her car with the trash bags. "Can't open the trunk," he said. "Looks like you got rear-ended."

"Yeah, somebody hit my car in the middle of the night last week. Hopefully everything will fit in the back."

"I'll make it fit." He opened the door, pushed and shoved the bags in, then forced the door closed. "There we go."

Her entire life fit into the backseat of an old, blue Civic.

"Miss Sullivan." Captain Brandt came over. "We're about ready to go."

"Okay."

"Do you have a place to stay?" he asked. "Family nearby?"

"No, but I'll figure something out." Patty pictured her nutty friends. Most of them were couch-surfing or living with their parents.

The captain pushed his glasses up the bridge of his nose. "All right then, I'm sure your landlord will get in touch with you. Listen, if you have any questions, you can call me." He pulled a business card from his shirt pocket and handed it to her.

"That's nice of you." She liked him again.

"Well, good luck." He hoisted himself into the truck. "You take care, now."

"Right. Thanks."

She stared at the fire engine in a daze. The motor started up, and the truck edged away from the curb. It rumbled down the street and disappeared.

Cars whizzed by—people on their way to work, taking kids to school, running errands. Everybody had somewhere to go, things to do, places to be.

Too busy to notice the red-headed girl standing in front of her red-tagged house with nowhere to go.

2

She sat in her car with the motor running, staring straight ahead, waiting for a guardian angel to appear and tell her what to do.

Then one did. Her cell chimed, and her best friend's face lit up the screen.

"Hey there, missy." It was Cece's usual greeting.

Patty burst into tears. "I'm homeless and I almost died!" She blubbered through the story of her destroyed kitchen and terrifying brush with death.

Her friend ordered her to drive up north immediately.

"Are you sure?"

"Of course I'm sure. You haven't been here since January. But are you okay to drive?"

"I think so." She held out her hands. They shook like an off-kilter washing machine.

"If you get on the road now, you'll be here before dark. I'll take care of you for a few days and help you figure things out. See you tonight."

"You're a lifesaver." Another round of tears flowed at the comforting thought of being near Cece.

Traffic came to a standstill in Santa Barbara.

Patty pulled off the freeway and drove to a mini-cot. Her head pounded from a lack of caffeine. She needed coffee—and junk food. Her resolution to eat healthfully had been abandoned months ago.

At the half-way point, near San Luis Obispo, she opened a package of Oreos.

By the time the Golden Gate Bridge came into view, she'd eaten all the cookies, a bag of Cheetos, and a package of Milk Duds. Her car was littered with wrappers, and her stomach was queasy.

At the foot of the bridge, a thick fog swallowed the road in front of her. She drove cautiously and stayed in the middle lane, for fear a truck might swerve and toss her little car over the side. At the end of the bridge, she exhaled and released her clenched jaw.

It was almost dark when Patty arrived in Clearwater, a picturesque town at the edge of Sonoma County. The quiet road took her past wineries with row upon row of grapevines, small inns nestled between giant oak trees and flower gardens, and homes set back at the end of long driveways.

She pulled into the driveway of Cece and Brad's house, a gray Cape Cod situated on a woody acre walking distance from the lake.

The front door flew open, and Cece ran down the steps. She wrapped her long arms around her. "Oh my God, I'm so happy to see you."

Patty buried her face in her friend's long, curly brown hair. Her legs buckled, but Cece held tight.

They clung to each other.

"Come on. Dinner's almost ready."

"You cooked for me? That's so nice."

"Of course I did. Lemme grab your…" Cece opened the car door and released an avalanche of shoes and clothing. "No suitcase?"

"It broke." Patty sniffled and sucked in her lower lip.

"Don't worry." Cece tossed everything back in and pushed the door closed. "We'll deal with it later."

They walked arm-in-arm up into the house.

Patty lifted her nose. "Oh, did you make roast chicken?"

"Yes I did, missy."

She hugged her again. "You're the best. What would I ever do without you?"

"That's a question you need never ask. Now go wash up. Dinner's almost ready."

A half-hour later, Patty, freshly showered and wearing an oversized terrycloth robe, entered the newly remodeled kitchen. The aroma of a homecooked meal greeted her.

"Hungry?" Cece put a platter of chicken and crispy potatoes on the center island.

"Starving." She pulled out a stool and sat "Where is everyone?"

"Noah's asleep, and Brad's at a meeting, so it's just us. We can stay up and talk into the wee hours like we used to."

"That sounds wonderful."

Patty leaned against her friend. Comfort radiated off her like warmth from a fire.

They'd met at UCLA when she'd been a freshman, and Cece a junior. For Patty, it was as if she'd found a soulmate.

They were the epitome of opposites who attract. She'd been a tiny tomboy, and Cece a tall, graceful dancer.

Within a few weeks of knowing each other, they'd moved into an apartment and remained roommates for the next eight years.

Patty had never been happier or more content. Their Yin and Yang friendship suited them both. Cece took care of everything that mattered, while Patty made sure they had fun.

But three years ago, Cece left Los Angeles. She returned to her hometown to pursue her passion—teaching ballet. Then she'd married Brad, the man of her dreams. Now she had a career, a husband, a house, and a baby.

At thirty-two, Cece had a grown-up life.

Patty, on the other hand, did not. A late bloomer from the start, she drifted through life like an unmanned boat on a lake.

The roast chicken with crispy skin tasted delicious, but Patty had trouble eating more than a few bites. She nibbled a piece of potato.

"I thought you were hungry."

"I thought I was, too. But my stomach's a little off." Patty's left eye twitched.

"And what's wrong with your eye? I've never seen it do that before."

"It's my nervous tic from when I was a kid. It came back." She pushed on the corner of her eye.

"You mean since this morning?"

"No. Since three months ago."

"Ah," Cece said. "Your dad's funeral."

Patty nodded. "The past three months have really beat me up."

"Do you want to talk about it?" her friend asked with a worried frown.

She shook her head. Going home for her father's funeral had been the hardest thing she'd ever done, and it was no surprise she didn't do it well. "I'm afraid you'll think less of me."

"No matter what you did that was so bad, I will *not* think less of you. I promise."

"Okay." Patty inhaled. She placed her fork on the edge of her plate and took a sip of water. "It started with a call from…"

3

It was a chilly morning in February when the call came. Patty was sitting at Starbucks, sipping a latte before going to a job interview down the street.

The screen said *Maggie*, so she tapped *decline*. Calls from her older sister were annoying and usually started with, "*Why can't you ever…*"

When her sister kept calling, Patty gave in.

"Hi, Maggie. What's up?" She took a sip of latte.

"You need to come home." Her sister's voice, normally authoritative, trembled.

"What's wrong?"

"Daddy had a heart attack this morning. He died."

The paper cup slid out of her hand and hit the floor, splattering coffee on her new white sneakers.

Maggie picked her up at the airport in a shiny new SUV.

Even with swollen eyes and no make-up, her sister was beautiful. Her blonde hair was pulled back into a messy ponytail, her fair skin smooth and pink.

Other than perfunctory hellos, neither sister said a word until Maggie glanced at Patty's outfit—sweats, black sneakers, and a baseball cap. "I hope you brought something appropriate to wear to the funeral."

"I did." She toyed with her necklace, sliding the silver moon charm along the chain. "How's Mom doing?"

"Terrible. The boys haven't left her side."

The boys were their brothers, twins born a year after Maggie and five years before Patty. "Their sycophantic hovering makes me nuts. And poor Liza can't stop crying."

Liza, the baby at twenty-one, looked exactly like Maggie, but their similarity ended there.

Liza was nice.

How Patty had landed in her family was a mystery. Her four siblings were tall, blond, and brilliant—three advantages Patty lacked. Between her small stature and fiery red hair, she stood out like a parrot among penguins.

If it not for an old photo of her grandmother, she would've believed her brothers' taunts that she'd been found in a box on the back steps.

Maggie's long fingers gripped the steering wheel.

"So, new car?" Patty asked.

"Yes. A gift for my thirty-fifth birthday." It sounded like bragging, but she wasn't like that. She was just direct and honest.

"How nice," she said. She hadn't meant to sound snippy, but her words were sharp around the edges.

"How long are you staying?" her sister asked.

"Not sure. I just grabbed the first one-way flight available that didn't cost a fortune."

Maggie sighed. "I'll pay for your flight."

She couldn't tell if her sister was being kind or controlling.

"It's okay, I can manage." What difference would another few hundred on the credit card make?

Patty had a grand plan to pay it off in one fell swoop as soon as she won the lottery. Until then, minimum payments would have to do.

The house was dark when they walked in.

She half expected to hear her father's voice, the slight Irish accent.

Ah, there's my Patty-cakes! He'd always say.

Maggie flipped on a light, and the sweet memory vanished.

"Where's Mom and Liza?" Patty asked.

"It's after midnight here. They're probably asleep." Her sister opened the refrigerator. She sniffed a carton of milk and lifted the foil on a casserole.

"What are you doing?"

"Just checking." Maggie closed the refrigerator. "We have to be at church by nine, so I'll pick you guys up at eight-thirty. Please be ready." She gave Patty a hasty kiss on the cheek and left.

As harsh as her sister was, her ability to manage everyone and everything had its advantages. What Patty couldn't stand about her sister—her bossy, overbearing authority—was what she needed. She depended on it.

Patty rolled her wobbly bag down the hall. She peeked into her parents' bedroom.

Liza and her mother were asleep in the bed her mom and dad had shared for nearly forty years.

She gently closed the door.

In her childhood bedroom, she changed into her nightshirt. She crossed the hall to the bathroom, vaguely aware of how familiar the old carpeting felt underneath her bare feet.

Patty brushed her teeth and washed her face, using a faded blue washcloth.

The yellow comforter on the twin bed was as old as she was.

Maybe older. She pulled it back, crawled in between the sheets, and fell into a restless sleep.

~

The funeral took place in the church where Patty had grown up. Throughout the service, she held her father's money clip, rubbing the cool metal with her thumb.

The priest droned on and on, his words unintelligible and meaningless.

She sat at the far end of the row with Liza to her right. Her younger sister stared straight ahead, tears rolling down her cheeks.

Patty scooted closer and pressed the money clip into her sister's hand with a gentle squeeze.

After the funeral, friends and neighbors filled the house.

The smell of food, the sound of quiet conversation, and the heat of too many bodies sickened Patty.

She ran to the bathroom and splashed her face with cold water. The feeling passed. When she stepped into the hallway, Maggie was standing in front of her.

"What's wrong?"

"Nothing." She headed into the bedroom.

"What're you doing?" Her sister grabbed her arm.

"I have to leave."

"Are you kidding? You just got here."

"I know, but I feel like the walls are closing in on me." She pressed her hands against her chest.

The door opened a crack, and Liza peeked in. "Is everything okay?"

"No." Maggie pulled her into the room. "Your favorite sister's leaving."

"You're not really, are you?"

Patty's heart raced. "I'm sorry."

Maggie threw her arms into the air. "My God, Patty, I hope someday you learn to face challenges, because believe me, life is full of them." She stormed out, slamming the door.

Liza's blue eyes glistened, and the tears on her long lashes looked like crystals. "Don't go. I need you."

"I can't do this." She put a hand on her throat, as if the words choked her. "It's too hard."

"It's hard for me, too." Her sister's voice broke. "But don't you think Daddy would want us to be together?"

Their father had adored his two late-in-life daughters.

"You know me, Liza. You know I'm useless."

"You're not useless. You just feel like you don't belong."

It was true. Patty was an outsider in her own family.

"Please, just stay one more day."

Her sister's sweet, soft voice swayed her. She closed her eyes and inhaled. "Okay."

"Thank you," her sister whispered.

Together, they rejoined the crowd in the over-heated living room.

Her mother was sitting on the couch with the twins, both in black suits, on either side of her like bookends.

She steeled herself and approached. "Mom?"

Her mother, wearing a stylish navy dress and a long strand of pearls, looked up. She pushed her blonde bangs to the side. "Oh, Patricia."

"Can I get you anything?"

She toyed with her wedding ring, and her gaze settled on her daughter's feet. "Did you wear tennis shoes to church?"

Patty stiffened. When it came to their relationship, maternal criticism was as natural as small talk. She'd spent years ignoring the comments. By the time she was fifteen, she provoked them. Whatever she could do to set herself apart from her perfect siblings, she'd done it.

"Do you want something to eat?" she asked, ignoring the shoe question.

"I'm fine," her mother said. "Your brothers are tending to me."

Patty bit her lower lip. She'd been dismissed. The corner of her left eye twitched. She pressed on it. The nervous tic that had disappeared when she moved to California was back.

That night, she and Liza looked through old photo albums, finding mostly pictures of their three older siblings but a few of themselves, too—special occasions like Christmas and Easter and birthday parties.

The arrangement in every family photo was consistent. On one side was their mother with the twins and Maggie. On the other side was their father with Baby Liza in his arms. As if an after-thought, Patty was on the end—her hair as visible as a clown's wig.

She didn't remember if someone had put her there or if she'd chosen the position herself.

Either way, the photo would've been better without her in it.

After going through three fat albums, they crawled into their childhood beds in the bedroom they'd shared for ten years.

Patty lay on her back and stared at a ray of moonlight as it wandered across the ceiling and, after a few hours, faded away.

At sunrise, she dressed and packed her bag.

Liza rolled over. "Are you leaving?"

She nodded. "My flight's in a couple hours. We'll talk soon," she said, although they probably wouldn't.

Liza had to get back to Princeton, Patty had to find a job, and everyone would return to their ordinary lives.

"Okay. Bye, Patty." Her sister's voice held no animosity, only sadness. She turned over and faced the wall.

She kissed Liza's cheek. "Bye."

Patty pulled her bag with the wobbly wheel into the entry

way and checked her phone. The Uber driver wouldn't arrive for a few more minutes.

She walked back toward her mother's room. She was poised to knock when everything went blurry.

Her heart pounded, and a swooshing sound filled her head. She struggled to breathe. Panic gripped her. She was about to die of a heart attack just like her dad.

Patty turned and ran.

She grabbed her suitcase and flew out of the house.

The driver pulled up a moment later, and she leapt into the car.

As they drove away, her panic subsided. Her breathing steadied. She wasn't going to die, unless one could die from shame.

Cece's mouth hung open. "You left without even saying goodbye to your mom?"

Patty "I told you it was bad."

"Bad, yes. But not unforgivable. Everybody grieves in their own way, sweetie, and you were grieving for your dad. You will be for a long time."

"I guess." She uncovered her face.

"Is your mom still mad at you?"

"I don't think she was ever really mad. She said my behavior wasn't unexpected, and I always sink to the occasion."

Cece grimaced. "That's harsh."

"That's typical." She drank the rest of her wine. "I just wish I could go back and change everything."

Her friend put an arm around her. "You can't change the past. You can only do better going forward."

Patty stared at the wall. Not only was she not doing better, she wasn't even going forward. "Mind if we talk about something else?"

"Okay." Cece took a breath. "What happened with the guy you met on the plane?"

She shuddered. "Oh, no. Not that."

"Come on." Her former roomie held up her pinky. "Remember? No secrets ever."

"Fine." Patty stretched her legs. "Long story short, I sat down, he smiled, I smiled. He bought me a drink. And then another drink. He was so sweet, not to mention gorgeous, and a great listener. By the time we got to LA, I'd been swept off my feet."

"It sounds wonderful."

"Oh, it was, for about a month. Then one night we were out to dinner, and he got up to, I don't know, go to the bathroom or something. Anyway, he'd left his phone on the table, and when it vibrated, I looked at it."

"Oh, no."

"The text said, and I quote: '*Don't forget diapers on your way home, love ya'.*"

Cece's jaw dropped. "What'd you do?"

"I did what I always do. I ran out." Patty rubbed her face. "There'd been a hundred red flags. I was just too stupid to see them."

Her eyes drifted away from her friend's, as if she didn't want to been seen.

"You're not stupid, you're just—just floundering."

"Floundering." She laughed a bitter laugh, and it hurt. She'd been floundering for three years. "I miss the old days, back when we lived in our cute little house in Santa Monica. Everything was so much easier."

"Not really. Don't you remember we were broke half the time?"

"Were we?" Patty blinked. "I don't remember that at all. I just remember being happy."

Cece squeezed her. “We were very happy. And you were the best roommate ever.”

“Really?”

“Absolutely.”

The tears turned on like a faucet. Patty fell against her and sobbed.

4

The smell of coffee and bacon wafted down the hall and into her bedroom. Patty's eyes fluttered open, and warm morning light greeted her.

She loved the guest room, which she considered *her* room. It was off a hallway behind the kitchen with its own bathroom, a walk-in closet, and hardwood floors.

Two tall windows on either side of the bed looked out to the backyard. The bedding was white with accents of pale blues and greens.

Above the bed was a painting of the lake by her favorite artist, *Cecilia Rose Redmond.* Her best friend was a woman of many talents.

Patty crawled out from under the down comforter, pulled on a pair of socks, and went to the kitchen.

"Good morning." Cece filled a mug with coffee and cream and handed it to her. "How'd you sleep?"

"I slept okay until the nightmare. I dreamed a bathtub was chasing me."

"Did it have a face?"

"No. But I sensed it was evil." Patty ate a piece of bacon. Her appetite had improved since last night. "What day is today?"

"Friday. When do you have to be back at to work?"

"Not 'til Tuesday." Patty worked part-time at Pottery Barn. "If they don't give me more hours, I'll have to find a second job."

"What happened to making custom frames?"

"I don't like it anymore."

Cece twisted her mouth to the side. She'd told Patty a thousand times, *Do what you love then find a way to make money doing it.*

"Don't say it." She put up her hand. "I'll do something I love once I figure out what it is I love to do. In the meantime, I like Pottery Barn. I get to arrange stuff."

"You're good at arranging."

"Yeah, I am." Patty ate more bacon. "So, what're we doing today?"

"Well, I have to be at the studio at two o'clock for my intermediate pointe class." Cece was a highly-regarded instructor at the dance academy where she'd trained growing up. "So this morning, I'm taking you to yoga."

Patty buttered a piece of toast. "No, you're not."

"Come on. It'll be good for you."

"No it won't. I hate yoga."

The sound of Noah fussing came through the baby monitor.

"Ha, saved by the baby. I'm going to get my godson. And I'm not going to yoga." She sprinted upstairs, looking forward to the baby's cherubic face.

He stood in his crib, chubby hands gripping the railing. When he saw her, he grinned, showing four little teeth and melting her heart. "Ti-ti."

"Oh my gosh, you still know me!" Patty lifted him out of his crib. He had his father's dark hair and his mother's sapphire blue eyes.

As she changed his diaper, it struck her that twenty-four hours earlier she'd almost been killed. She shook off the chilling thought and carried Noah downstairs.

In the kitchen, she handed him to his mommy, who smothered him with kisses before buckling him into his highchair.

"Noah recognized me," Patty said.

"Of course he did. I show him your picture every night."

"You do not."

Cece put a bowl in the microwave. "Yeah, I do. I show him the picture of you holding him, the one on the dresser, and I say *Auntie Patty* over and over.

"Really? That's so sweet." Patty was about to refill her coffee, but a flash of black fur skirting across the kitchen stopped her. "Oh my God, did I just see a cat?"

"Yes, you did."

"But you don't like cats."

The black feline with white mittens slinked under the chair and around the table legs.

"I like Shadow. Besides, he's not ours. He belongs to Dawn, who's in New York with her dance company."

Dawn was Brad's eighteen-year-old daughter from his first marriage. At one time, she'd been Cece's star student.

"Nice of you to kitty-sit." Patty scratched Shadow between the ears. The cat purred with pleasure.

A timer pinged, and Cece pulled the bowl from the microwave. She stirred the cereal and handed it to Patty. "You can feed Noah while I get dressed, and then we're going to yoga."

"I am not going to yoga."

Her friend ruffled her hair. "Yes, you are."

Patty looked at the baby. "I'm not going to yoga."

Noah giggled and squished his hand in the cereal.

~

The yoga studio was full of mothers and babies. Diaper bags littered the floor.

"Are you serious?" Patty had on a white tank top, black sneakers, and a pair of her friend's too-large yoga pants. A tiny ponytail stuck out on the back of her head. "I look like an alien here. And you didn't tell me I needed to accessorize with a baby."

"You don't need a baby. Now come on." Cece shifted Noah to her other hip and led Patty to a blue mat on the floor. "You take this one."

A baby a few mats over shrieked.

Another baby fussed and wailed.

Noah's little face crinkled, as if in alliance with his compatriots. Within a minute, every baby in the room was crying.

"Don't worry, it always starts like this."

"Maybe the babies don't like yoga." Patty's eye twitched. "Listen, I'm not up to this. Okay with you if I just go for a walk?"

"Are you sure? I really think you'll like it once we get started."

She hated to disappoint Cece, but the warm room full of crying babies, one of which must've had a dirty diaper, was more than she could take. "Completely sure."

"All right, meet me at Nutmeg's in an hour. We'll have lattes and a sticky bun." She gave her a quick squeeze.

Outside the yoga studio, Patty leaned against the building. She held her hands out; they were shaking.

A long walk would do her good.

The town of Clearwater, awash in spring sunlight, welcomed. She turned the corner onto Main Street and took in the familiar surroundings.

The senior citizen walking club passed by with smiles and friendly hellos.

A cyclist waved as he sped past her.

The scent of cookies baking at Nutmeg's filled the air.

Workers were putting signs in shop windows announcing the upcoming Memorial Day celebration.

She crossed the street and followed a shady path into the park, an island of green grass, flower gardens, lush trees, and play areas in the center of town.

Up ahead, Patty spotted Trevor Castillo, her favorite barista at Nutmeg's.

He was on a ladder painting the round pavilion situated in the middle of the park.

"Hey Trev."

"Hey Patty! It's been a while." He came down and removed his painter's cap, uncovering a black man-bun. His face had dots of white paint on it.

"Yeah, I've had a lot going on." She told him about the bathtub incident.

"Boy, that sucks. What're you gonna do?"

"No idea," she said. "The only thing I know for sure is I'm meeting Cece for coffee in an hour. I hope you'll be at Nutmeg's by then."

"I'm off today. My one day off this week, and I'm here painting for my dad, who happens to be the new mayor. Every little thing that needs doing around here, he volunteers me to do it."

"Well, you are a jack-of-all-trades." She patted his arm.

"Can you believe he put me in charge of decorating the town square for Memorial Day? Hey, will you still be here? It's gonna be a fun weekend."

Patty shook her head. "That's like in two weeks. I'll be long gone by then."

"Too bad," Trevor said. "Well, come by Nutmeg's tomorrow. I'll make you your favorite." He flashed a charming smile, picked up his paintbrush, and went back to work.

Patty meandered through the park. The air smelled fresh and

smog-free. She stopped to say hello to Rebecca, the neighborhood dog-walker.

In overalls and blue sneakers, her reddish-brown hair in two messy pigtails, Rebecca looked like a farm girl from another era. "What's up, Patty?" She had five dogs with her—two labs, one poodle, a huge Saint Bernard, and a little brown mutt. "Visiting Cece and Brad again?"

"Just for a few days." She explained the bathtub saga again, finding a bit of comfort in the young woman's effusive sympathy.

"You know," Rebecca said. "Dogs are wonderful at helping people deal with trauma. You should totally get one."

Patty crouched and scratched the friendly brown mutt under his chin. She could hardly take care of herself let alone a pet. "Someday, maybe."

"Well, I gotta run. See you around, I hope." The adorable dog-walker waved and guided her pack across the lawn like a camp counselor.

Patty stood still, unsure of which way to go, a metaphor for her life.

At twenty-nine, she needed to take control of something instead of just letting things happen. Let go of the past, make better decisions, take charge of her life—it sounded so simple.

She sat on a bench under a tree with branches that stretched out in all directions creating a beautiful canopy of interwoven limbs.

Even trees knew what direction to take.

Patty's cellphone buzzed from her pocket, interrupting her analysis of trees. It was a text from a number she didn't recognize, but the message was clear.

Cece hurt come to yoga studio asap!

5

Patty ran like an Olympic sprinter.

Inside the studio, Cece sat on a bench surrounded by three women.

Noah, on the hip of somebody she didn't recognize, was wailing. When he saw Patty, he reached his arms out as if needing to be rescued.

The woman handed him over.

"What happened?" Patty asked, rubbing her godson's back.

Cece held her arm against her body. "I tripped on a mat," she said tearfully.

"Did you call 9-1-1?"

The woman who'd been holding Noah shook her head. "Don't be ridiculous—it's not an emergency. She just needs an X-ray."

"How do you know?" Patty asked.

"She's a doctor," Cece said, clearly in pain.

"Oh," Patty said, lowering her chin.

The door swung open, and Natalie Lurensky, Cece's childhood friend and owner of the ballet studio, blew in like Wonder Woman.

"What happened? Oh, Patty, hi!"

"Hi, Nat." Patty had always liked her.

The woman ran a successful business, cared for her elderly mother, and had a kind word for everyone she met.

The yoga teacher wrung her hands. "Thank God she wasn't holding the baby."

"I've got to go." The doctor picked up her yoga mat. "Can one of you take Cece for an X-ray?"

"I don't need an X-ray. I just need to go home and put ice on it."

"You do need one," the yoga teacher said.

"I don't," Cece pouted.

"You absolutely do," the doctor repeated.

Patty looked from woman to woman, as if watching a tennis match.

"She's right," Natalie said. "Come on, I'll take you."

The doctor flashed a satisfied smile. "Thank you, Natalie, always the sensible one. I'll call the clinic and tell them to expect you. And whatever you do, do not take that baby into the hospital. Too many nasty germs." She pushed open the glass door and left.

As Natalie helped Cece into the car, Patty jiggled Noah on her hip.

"Hey, why don't I stay here with the baby? You heard what the doctor said." It was the perfect excuse to avoid going to the hospital.

"You don't mind?" Cece asked, fumbling with the seatbelt. "He's gonna need lunch and changing and a nap. And I don't know how long we'll…"

"Don't worry. I can handle it." She closed the car door before her injured friend could change her mind.

~

The cast covered Cece's right arm from her fingers to her elbow.

Patty looked on sympathetically. She'd come away from her own disaster with nary a scratch, but poor Cece had broken her wrist in a simple slip and fall.

While Noah smeared spaghetti sauce around his tray and Patty cleared the dishes, Cece and Brad studied their laptops.

Brad, a forty-year-old lawyer, had dark brown hair, strong features, and a dimple in his chin. He was confident, kind, and honest to a fault. In lawyerly circles, they called him Atticus Finch.

Patty loved him almost as much as she loved Cece.

"I'll postpone my business trip," he said.

"I hate for you to do that," Cece said, still groggy from the pain medication.

"Can't Julia help?" Patty asked.

Julia was Cece's best-in-the-world stepmom.

"She and my dad are on a cruise. Won't be back until the end of the month."

Brad clicked on his keyboard. "I can go to New York in a couple weeks. It's not that big a deal."

"It *is* a big deal." Cece pointed to her screen. "Look. Dawn'll be in New York next week. It's your only chance to see her all summer."

"Shoot. That's right."

"Maybe it's time you hired a nanny," Patty said. "I mean, isn't that what everyone does?"

"I don't want a nanny." Cece leaned on her left elbow. "I manage fine when I have two working hands. It's just bad timing, with Julia and my dad away. They're our back-up."

"Whatever." She picked up Noah and carried him to the sink. "Hey, maybe your cleaning service has temporary babysitters."

Brad cleared his throat. "Patty, when do you have to get back to LA?"

"I'm leaving Monday," she said, running the baby's hands

under warm water. "I have an early shift Tuesday morning." She tore a paper towel off the roll.

Both Brad and Cece were looking at her with wide, expectant eyes.

"Oh. Oh, no." As much as she loved Noah, Patty was hardly equipped to play nanny. Plus, she had to get home and figure out whose couch she could crash on until her ceiling was fixed.

"Can you stay longer?" her friend asked. "Just until Brad gets back?"

It pained her to say no. "You know I would, but I just started this job. And because I'm part-time, if I don't work, I don't get paid. I'm really sorry."

"What do they pay you at Pottery Barn?" Brad asked.

"Oh my God." Cece smacked her husband's arm. "That's terrible."

"$14.80 an hour." Patty answered quicker than intended. She backpedaled, ashamed at herself for saying *'no'* in the first place. "Forget it. I'll stay, it's the least I can do, and I'd never let you pay me."

"Really?" Cece reached for her hand. "Are you sure?"

"Yeah, my boss is nice—I doubt he'll fire me. Or maybe he will." But her job was of less concern than her ability to care for a baby. She held Noah tightly, as if protecting him from herself. "What if I mess up? I'm an expert at letting people down. And you're the last two people in the world I'd want to disappoint."

"You'll do fine," Cece said.

"That's right," Brad said. "You need to have more faith in yourself."

More faith? In order to have more she needed to have some to start with.

"Well, I guess we can give it a try."

She had to admit it felt good to do something for her friends. Besides, staying in Clearwater was one way to avoid dealing with her living situation, or lack thereof.

"Thank you," Brad said, taking Noah from her. "And of course I'll pay you, if not in money, then in lattes and sticky buns and fine red wine."

"Isn't that how you lured Cece into marrying you?" She gave him a sly smile.

He returned the grin. "You bet."

Cece got weepy. She hugged Patty with her good arm. "You're a lifesaver."

Her friend's gratitude wrapped around her like a warm blanket.

6

On Monday morning, after Brad left for the airport, Patty began her new routine.

While Noah sat in his highchair eating Cheerios, she washed Cece's long brown hair in the kitchen sink. She towel-dried it then worked it into a thick French braid.

"All those years we lived together," Cece said, admiring her new hairstyle. "And I never knew your unique talent. How'd you learn to braid like this?"

"Are you forgetting I grew up with sisters? Doing each other's hair was on the chore wheel."

By the time the house was tidy and Noah down for a nap, Patty was exhausted. She'd had no idea that housework and running after a toddler, not to mention caring for a one-armed adult female, could be so draining.

She poured herself a glass of orange juice.

A moment later, Cece appeared in a black leotard. "Can you help me with my skirt?"

"Sure." Patty wrapped the skirt around Cece's waist and tied the bow. "How are you going to teach ballet with only one arm?"

"I'll figure it out," she said, tucking a pair of pink ballet slippers into her bag. "Do you want to walk into town with Noah later? We can grab an early dinner somewhere."

"Sounds good. Hey, are you sure you can drive?"

"We'll see, won't we?" She kissed Patty's cheek. "Thank you again for staying. You're the best."

Once Cece was gone, Patty flopped on the couch with a piece of leftover pizza and Shadow purring against her leg. She scrolled through TV shows, stopping on *Fixer Upper*, but the construction site reminded her of the bathtub sitting in her kitchen at her red-tagged apartment. She flipped channels and found *Law and Order*.

After two episodes of crimes neatly solved and bad guys put away, she went upstairs to check on Noah.

He was sound asleep on his tummy, his legs tucked underneath and his little diapered bottom in the air.

She sat in the rocker and watched him breathe. The steady rhythm calmed her.

Patty dozed. She dreamed about her father.

In the mid-afternoon sunshine, she pushed the stroller along the tree-lined streets of Clearwater while Noah pointed and babbled.

They walked through a playground where children were climbing on a jungle gym and digging in the sand. Parents sat on benches watching, talking, and snapping photos.

She went down the shady path, breathing in the scent of woodchips and honeysuckle.

Noah dropped his sippy cup on the ground.

Patty wiped the spout with her shirt and shook out a few drops of juice to clear dirt from the holes. She handed it back to the baby, and he stuck it in his mouth.

On Main Street they passed a needlepoint shop, a bookstore, a fruit market, and an old- fashioned ice cream parlor.

She went in and got herself a strawberry milkshake. Nothing better than a tasty milkshake on a lovely spring day.

"Mmm," she said to Noah, sipping on the straw. "Want some?"

He opened his mouth like a baby bird.

Patty poured a little into his sippy cup and smiled as he tipped it back and slurped. The spout popped out of his mouth, and Noah grinned, pink liquid dribbling down his chin.

"You are the cutest thing ever." Patty wiped his chin and continued walking.

She stopped in front of one of her favorite places, Mariano's Cheese and Wine. "How about we go inside and visit Tessa?"

Noah bounced and said something that sounded like *cheese*.

She opened the door, jingling the bells on the knob, and maneuvered the stroller inside.

On the left side of the shop was a refrigerated case packed with wheels and wedges of specialty cheeses. The counter above it was laden with cheese samples, assorted crackers, and other tasty bites. On the opposite wall were floor to ceiling shelves full of wines from all over the world and a massive selection of gourmet food. Olives, pickled vegetables, sausage, smoked fish, caviar, sweets—everything one would need for a romantic picnic at the lake.

Patty raised her nose and sniffed. The shop smelled like bread just out of the oven.

"Tessa? Are you here?"

"Is that you, Patty?" The shop owner called from the storeroom.

"Me and Noah."

"Stay put. I'll be right out."

"Okay." Patty tasted a few cheese samples and gave Noah a bite of mild cheddar.

A loud bang, like a cabinet door slamming, made her jump.

"I told you three times, I'm not interested."

Patty popped an olive into her mouth.

"Come on Tessa, a trial run, that's all I ask." The voice was deep and commanding. "I'll help you do the rearranging."

"I can't just toss off the others to make room for you."

"Last week you said you'd think about it."

"I did think about it. And now I'm done thinking about it."

The door between the storeroom and the shop swung open. Tessa came out followed by a man carrying a box.

He looked to be in his thirties, with chestnut brown hair and a beard that was a shade lighter.

Patty stepped back, taking in his muscular arms and broad shoulders.

"And for God's sake." He put the box on the counter and pointed to a display of bottles. "Why are you carrying this red blend crap from Paso?"

"Because it's excellent, Adam." Tessa stood beside the bottles, as if to protect them. She was petite with a curvy figure, short dark hair, wispy bangs, and wide-set brown eyes framed by long lashes. "I sell a lot of it, too."

Adam pressed his lips into a thin line, his scruffy beard hiding his mouth. He reached up, exposing a small tattoo that looked like twisted vines on the inside of his right wrist, and removed a stemmed glass from the rack hanging from the ceiling.

Patty sipped the milkshake, her lips tight on the straw, aware of his rugged masculinity.

Adam uncorked a bottle of his wine with a satisfying pop, filled the glass, and swirled the dark purple liquid.

"Look at it." He held it up to the light. "My Syrah is the best in the region, probably in all of California."

"I'm sorry." Tessa crossed her arms. "My shelves are full. I've signed contracts."

He set the wine glass on the counter in front of Patty. "You're making a mistake. This wine will be an award winner by end of summer."

"We'll see about that."

A wry smile formed around the edges of the man's mouth. He shook his head. "It's been years, Tessa. Time for you to let go." He picked up his box and walked out.

"Jerk!" She called after him.

"What was that about?" Patty couldn't wait to hear, but the shop owner waved away the question.

"Nothing important." She kissed Patty on both cheeks. "I'm so happy to see you. I heard you were almost squashed under a tub."

"Yeah, lucky to be alive, I suppose." She lifted the glass of wine, stuck her nose in and inhaled. "So what's between you and that guy? You don't like his wine?"

"You tell me."

She took a sip, held it in her mouth like she'd seen it done on TV, then swallowed. "Well, I'm no expert, and I was just drinking a milkshake." Patty sipped again. "But if I have to guess, I'd say it's good. Really good."

Tessa gave her an approving nod. "You're right. It's excellent. But I can't stand Adam."

"Why not?" Patty kind of liked him already. Although, her recent history proved she wasn't the best judge of men.

"There was an incident a few years ago." The shop owner took Noah out of the stroller and kissed his head.

Patty boosted herself onto a stool. "An incident?"

"Yes. And then an argument. And then a falling out. And then the damage was done." Tessa ate a cracker and gave the baby a piece. "Anyway, that's really all I can say."

Patty respected her professional discretion. "I get it. Business is business."

Tessa gave her a sidelong glance. "Yes, it is."

"The wine's really good though." Patty pointed at the glass.

"I know. And definitely in demand."

"Sounds like a classic case of cutting off your nose to spite your face."

"Probably." Tessa pursed her lips. "But we Italians, once crossed, don't forget. Didn't you ever see *The Godfather*?"

"Yikes." Patty laughed. "Remind me never to cross you."

"You couldn't possibly." She shifted Noah to her other hip. "So, how long are you staying this time?"

"A few more days. Cece broke her arm at the…"

"Yoga studio, I know," Tessa said, shaking her head. "Such a dangerous place. Is it any wonder I don't do yoga?"

"Right?" Patty held her hands out, indicating the danger should be obvious to everyone. "That's what I said. Anyway, I'm helping out with Noah until Brad gets home. By then, I probably can move back into my apartment. I hope. I mean, how long can it take to repair a ceiling?

"I'm sure it'll all work out," Tessa said, as if sensing her concern.

"Yeah, me too."

"Then again, it might not. My father used to say this thing in Italian, loosely translated, as '*not all donuts come out with a hole.*'"

"I have no idea what that means." Patty took Noah and put him back in the stroller. "But it doesn't sound good."

"You know, things go awry. All I'm saying is that life is full of surprises—some good, some not."

"No kidding. I'm the girl who just had a thousand pounds of porcelain fall through her ceiling."

"Exactly," Tessa held up the glass of Hawk and Winter's Syrah, as if toasting her insight. She swallowed the rest of the wine. "Life is unpredictable, that's just a fact. We never know what will happen next."

Patty shivered. If there was one thing the falling bathtub taught her, it was that.

7

The next day, Tessa's prophesy that plans tend to go awry, came to be. There'd been no news from her landlord, so Patty called Captain Brandt and left him a message.

His text came a few hours later while she was in the kitchen making tuna sandwiches for lunch.

Drove by apt nothing going on. Still wrapped in tape. Will try to find out more.

"Oh no."

"What's wrong?" Cece asked, trying to wipe her son's dirty face with her left hand.

Patty showed her the text. "It's been almost a week. What could be taking so long?"

"Construction takes time, " her friend said. "But you can stay here as long as you need."

"I don't know about that." Patty licked a bit of mayonnaise

off her thumb. "It's one thing to be here a week or so; I can't stay forever."

"It won't be forever. Landlords need tenants or they don't make any money."

"I know, but if I don't get back to work soon, I'll probably get fired, and even though I said I didn't care, I kinda do. And if that happens, I'll be homeless *and* unemployed." Patty sniffled. "I'll have to live in my car with a trunk that won't open."

"Now you're being ridiculous."

It wasn't ridiculous at all. Her only other option was to go back home to Texas.

The twitch in her eye switched on like a light.

A few days after the text from Captain Brandt, Patty went with Cece and Noah to Nutmeg's. They sat at a round table on the patio under an umbrella.

She was a mess of nerves. Her landlord still hadn't returned her call, and the fire captain had no new information.

Her stomach churned. She picked the pecans out of her sticky bun.

"You're making a mess out of that." Cece pulled the plate away.

"Sorry. I'm not very hungry."

"I know you're worried about the apartment." She picked up a toy her son had dropped. "Still no news from your fireman friend?"

Patty shook her head. "I feel so helpless, like I should be doing something, but I don't know what I'm supposed to do."

When Patty and Cece had been roommates, Cece had always taken care of the hard stuff. Over three years since they'd lived together, and Patty still was struggling to adjust.

Trevor came by with a fresh latte. “It’s decaf.” He wore a worried smile.

“Thanks.”

Everyone was being so nice to her.

Patty sipped her coffee and pictured the stuff she’d left in her apartment. She didn’t need any of it. It was disturbing how easily she’d dismantled and stepped away from her life, as if she had no roots holding her in place.

She jumped when someone patted her on the back.

“Hello!” Tessa popped up with a gigantic, panting Saint Bernard. “You’re a little jittery today, aren’t you?”

“With good reason,” Patty said. “Is that your dog?”

“Sort of. Buttercup actually belongs to my son, but you know how those things go. Kids promise they’ll take care of the pet, and then everything falls on the mother.”

Buttercup rested her head on Patty’s leg. She stroked the dog’s soft fur. It was oddly comforting. Maybe Rebecca was right about her needing a dog.

The shop owner pulled up a chair. “Now tell me, why the glum face?”

Patty admitted to Tessa that her prediction had come to pass—things were *not* working out. “So now I’m homeless.”

Cece scoffed. “You’ll never be homeless.”

“Maybe.” She fiddled with the charm on her necklace. “But I doubt Brad wants me living with you forever. Besides that, I need to make money. I might be living rent-free, but I still have bills to pay.”

“You really should let us pay you for helping out with Noah. Don’t be so stubborn.”

“Absolutely not. Noah’s my godson. It’s my honor and duty to care for him.”

Her friends looked at her as if she’d just delivered a moving sermon.

“Now there’s a good friend,” Tessa said.

"I'll say." Cece smiled. "The best."

"Well, it's the truth." Patty voice shook.

"But you're right," Tessa said. "You still need an income."

Patty chewed the inside of her cheek. "Hey, is there a Pottery Barn around here? Maybe I could transfer."

"Nope." Tessa shook her head. "Closest one is at least forty miles away. How about you come work for me?"

"That's crazy. I know nothing about wine and cheese."

"Actually, your assessment of the wine the other day was right on the money. Besides, whatever you need to know I'll teach you."

Patty pouted. "You just feel sorry for me, don't you?"

"Actually, no. Okay, maybe a little. But the truth is my regular assistant is taking the summer off, so I'm looking for someone. Might as well be you. It pays fifteen an hour. Will that work?"

Twenty cents more than Pottery Barn. "It would," Patty admitted, "but I still don't know how long I'm here. Once Cece has her arm back, I…"

Tessa waved off her objections. "A few weeks, a month, whatever. We'll make it work."

Patty hemmed. "But I still have Noah. He's my priority."

"We'll plan your schedule accordingly. I'm very flexible."

The offer sounded simple, but it added pressure to an already complicated situation.

What if she did a bad job?

What if she couldn't handle the responsibility?

What if she hated the work?

Patty pressed on the corner of her eye. "So, you'd be my boss. That might be weird."

Tessa scratched her dog's ears. "Then consider me your mentor. I'm an excellent teacher."

Cece nudged Patty's arm. "You're overthinking. It's not that big of a commitment, and Tessa's right—we can make the schedule work."

She shifted her gaze between her friends. They both needed her, and that made Patty nervous. Still, she had to earn *some* money. And it was only temporary, so if it didn't work out, no big deal. "Okay, then. I'll do it."

8

When she wasn't looking after Noah or helping Cece wash her hair and get dressed, Patty was busy at Mariano's Cheese and Wine.

Working in the gourmet shop turned out to be much more interesting than she'd expected.

Her mentor was not only an astute business woman; she was one of the most in demand sommeliers in Sonoma. Several nights a week, she taught wine-pairing classes and hosted tastings with local wineries.

The evening events were perfect for Patty's schedule. She could set up during the afternoon, run home to help Cece with Noah, and return to the shop until nine or ten at night.

Being busy was a blessing and exhausting. For the first time since her father's funeral, she slept like a log.

Memorial Day weekend brought early tourists into town for the two-day celebration. It began Saturday afternoon on the town square, where Trevor had decorated the pavilion with streamers, balloons, and American flags. All of Clearwater came out for the pet parade, old-fashioned lawn games, and farmers market.

Mariano's had a booth near the pavilion and directly across

the street from the shop. Visitors flocked around Tessa to hear her talk about wine, wine-making, and wineries in the area. While her new boss chatted, Patty was busy preparing a fancy cheese and fruit tray. She'd been working at the shop for two weeks, and had become an expert at making enticing platters.

When the crowd thinned, Tessa opened the large cooler on wheels. "We're about out of Chardonnay," she said. "Hold down the fort while I go get a few more bottles."

"Why don't I go?"

"I'm not sure which ones I want. Besides, I have to get Buttercup. My ex-husband is dropping her off. Don't worry, you'll be fine."

"I'm not so sure. I probably know just enough to get myself into trouble."

"You know more than you think." She headed toward the shop.

"Okay." Patty smoothed her white apron. She hoped nobody would ask her about anything other than cheese and olives and fancy tapenade.

People passed by with smiles and hellos.

She had plenty of samples on the tray, so she sat and gave her feet a rest. She picked up one of the brochures and studied the map of wineries in and around Clearwater.

"Excuse me."

Patty jumped up.

A man and woman stood in front of her.

"Hi!" She lifted the cheese tray. "Would you like some cheese? This French brie is excellent."

Please don't ask me about wine, please please please...

"Actually," the man said. "We were wondering about a particular wine."

She put on a fake smile. "Okay, um, red or white?"

The man and woman laughed as if she were joking, so she laughed, too.

Maybe she could stall until Tessa returned.

"We carry many different wines. And excellent gourmet foods." Patty opened a jar of sweet red pepper spread. "May I offer you a sample of…"

"No, thanks," said the woman. "We're just interested in the wine. It's a Cabernet, and somebody told us the winery is near here. Or somewhere in Sonoma."

That narrows it.

There were over four hundred wineries in Sonoma. She picked up the brochure with the map. "Maybe this will help."

A man wearing jeans, a blue T-shirt that hugged his torso, a Giant's baseball cap, and sunglasses stopped to look at the wines on display. In his free hand he held a leash that had a brown mutt attached to it. The dog's snout was a bit off center, as if his nose had slipped to the side.

"Hello," the man said to no one in particular.

The woman gave him a vague smile then turned her attention back to Patty. "Anyway, we were hoping you could help us figure out what winery we might be looking for. They have tastings, I know that."

Well that narrows it even more.

"And dogs." The man held up a finger, as if he'd just identified the most important fact. "Our friend said they played with two dogs. Great Danes, I think."

"That'll be BenderSmith," the man with the brown mutt said. "Just over the hill on Tuscan Road." He opened the brochure and pointed. "You're here in this green area, and BenderSmith is right there. About a ten-minute drive. Tell them Adam Hawk sent you." He pulled a business card out of his pocket.

Adam Hawk?

Patty held her breath, worried Tessa would return and get into an argument with him.

The woman accepted the card. "Is this your winery?"

"It is." He extended his hand.

The tattoo on his wrist caught Patty's attention.

"Hawk and Winters."

"We'd love to taste your wines, too." The man shook Adam's hand. "We're rather new to collecting and could use a little education."

"I'd be happy to pour for you. If you're around tomorrow after the fair, come by. I'll be in the tasting room."

The couple said they would. They thanked Patty and walked away, leaving her alone with Adam Hawk and the little brown dog.

He obviously had no memory of her. "You work for Tessa?" he asked, removing his sunglasses.

"Well, sort of, just temporarily. I, um…" She closed her mouth and cleared her throat. "Yes."

Adam nodded, as if mulling over her answer. "Cool." His eyes were gray-blue, like pebbles under water. His beard had grown fuller since the day he was in Tessa's shop. It gave him a rugged mountain-man look.

Patty opened her mouth then closed it. She almost mentioned their prior encounter but didn't. "That was nice of you to help out that couple."

"Just answered a question, that's all. Mind if I taste the cheese?"

She held out the tray.

"Thanks." He took four toothpicks at once, then put three samples into his mouth and gave the fourth to his dog.

Patty was about to ask if he liked it, but Tessa was walking toward them with Buttercup, a scowl on her face.

"That cheese is way too expensive for a dog. Not even Buttercup gets to sample it."

Adam raised one eyebrow. "Hello, Tessa."

They looked at each other as if in a standoff, but their dogs greeted each other like old friends.

"Did you need something?" she asked.

"No. Just having a little chat here." He nodded in Patty's direction.

The tension between them felt like a wall of cold air.

"Actually," Patty said. "Adam was able to answer a question for a couple that came by. About a winery they wanted to visit."

"They were looking for the Danes," he said.

Tessa's frown relaxed. "BenderSmith?"

She jumped to answer. "Yes! Adam gave them directions." She sounded overly chipper, as if the directions were a prize.

Tessa and Adam eyed each other.

Patty tried to interpret their stances.

Both were firmly planted, unwilling to say the next word. Their silence was unnerving.

To her relief, the little brown mutt barked and pulled the leash, distracting his owner.

Adam stepped back. "All right, Tips, let's go." He sauntered off, his broad shoulders stretching the seams of his shirt.

"I know what you're thinking."

Tessa's voice brought her back to reality.

"I'm not thinking anything." She defended herself. "Nothing. Zero. Complete blank."

"You think he's nice, I can tell." Tessa's brown eyes narrowed, her long lashes lowering like a dark curtain. "And handsome."

"No, I—well, yeah. He is handsome, and he was nice until you got back. Like really nice."

An amused smile spread across Tessa's face. "He certainly can be. I just know too much. So, we'll leave it at that. If you want to be friends with Adam Hawk, that's up to you." She opened the cooler. "Just remember, Hawk and Winters Wines will never stand on my shelves."

Was that information, or a warning?

~

That evening, as the sun was setting, Patty met Cece and Noah in front of the pavilion to watch the chili taste-off.

Brad, one of the esteemed judges, sat on stage at a long table with the other tasters. He appeared to be taking his responsibility seriously, as if each spoonful of chili were a sip of expensive wine.

They sat on the grass with Noah crawling around them.

"I'm so happy you're here," Cece said, bumping her shoulder. "And that's not because you've changed my son's diapers, given him umpteen baths, and washed and braided my hair."

"I know." Patty urged the toddler into her lap. "But I feel like less of a freeloader when you need me."

"I'll always need you, missy." She squeezed her hand.

"And me you." Patty squeezed back.

A deafening boom rang out, and the high school band marched by with drums beating.

The sound grabbed Noah's attention. He crawled toward the music. On the verge of walking for weeks, he tried to stand. The toddler wobbled, fell forward, squatted, and tried again.

On his chubby legs and bare feet, he rose up, lifted one foot, and moved it forward. The music swelled, and Noah took another step, as if the sound propelled him forward. Everyone stopped to watch Cece and Brad Redmond's baby take his first steps. *Stars and Stripes Forever* blasted throughout the park.

Brad ran down the pavilion steps, knelt on one knee, and opened his arms. Noah, his smile wide and wet, took three steps, stumbled to the side, rolled over, and got back on his feet. The crowd erupted with applause as father scooped son up and threw him into the air.

Cece sprinted toward her family.

Patty was about to follow her, but she stopped herself. It was a moment in which she didn't belong.

~

Patty crawled into bed and turned off the light, hoping sleep would come quickly and shut down her brain. An itch on her foot; rustling leaves outside; drip-drip-drip coming from the bathroom.

She got up and tightened the shower knobs then closed the window and got back into bed. Still, sleep eluded her.

Maybe a snack would help.

As she approached the doorway into the kitchen she heard Cece and Brad talking.

She was about to join them, but when Cece said her name she stopped and perked up her ears.

"Do you think I'm preventing Patty from dealing with her troubles?"

"Why would you think that?" her husband asked.

"Because she's in limbo. She had a crisis, and I should be helping her deal with it. Instead, I break my stupid wrist and end up needing her. I feel like I'm taking advantage of her situation."

Patty pressed her back to the wall.

"I think it's a win-win," he said. "You need her, and she needs you. Frankly, both of you are benefitting from each other's predicaments."

Hmmm. That is true.

"And you're not keeping her from dealing with anything. She'll deal with her troubles when she's ready." There was a pause. "Or when she has no other choice."

Patty forgot about the snack and tiptoed back to her room. What Brad had said unnerved her. What did he mean by *no other choice*?

Her list of problems overwhelmed her. Everything from her condemned apartment to her string of bad boyfriends, to her troublesome family.

She got under the covers and pulled the quilt over her head.

9

JUNE

The days grew warmer and longer; the lake attracted boaters and fishermen and teenagers on summer vacation.

Patty's landlord finally returned her call and said the repair work would begin soon. The call boosted her mood—at least things were heading in the right direction.

The weekend after Memorial Day, Phil and Julia Camden, Cece's parents, finally returned.

Patty couldn't wait to see them. She adored Phil and Julia. They'd welcomed her into the Camden family ages ago, the first time she'd visited Clearwater with Cece.

Also, she needed Julia's help with Noah.

In only one week, the little guy had gone from clumsy walking to almost running. He had a large goose-egg in the middle of his forehead where his face had smacked the floor.

Looking after a toddler was exhausting and terrifying.

Within hours of dropping their suitcases off at home, Cece's parents arrived at the Redmond house for Sunday family dinner.

Amidst hugs and kisses and much excitement, Patty observed the family dynamic, so opposite her own.

Phil tossed his grandson into the air. "Look at this big kid! Gonna be a football player just like your uncle, aren't you?"

Noah squealed in delight, his hands grasping his grandpa's graying beard.

"Phil, be careful," Julia said. "You're being too rough."

"Are you kidding? He loves it." The older man made a raspberry on the toddler's belly and sent him into another fit of giggles.

Five minute later, the door burst open and Tom, Cece's younger brother, bounded in.

"Hey you!" He wrapped Patty in a bear hug. "I'm glad you're alive."

"Thanks, Tommy." She squeezed the former football player.

They'd had a reckless romance a few years prior. It'd lasted all of sixteen days before imploding, a prediction made by Cece from the start. After a few months of avoiding each other, they'd gone back to being friends.

"Dinner's ready," Cece said, ushering everyone to the table.

Within a few minutes, the conversation switched from how much Noah had grown to the disaster that had befallen Patty.

As they ate barbequed steak and grilled vegetables, Phil and Tom, both electricians, peppered her with questions and speculation.

"Gotta be on top of old houses," Cece's brother said. "I see it all the time—bad wiring, leaks, termites, mold. Geez, Patty, you could've been killed."

"I know that." She didn't need a reminder of how close she'd come to being squashed like a bug.

"Hey, I'm just telling you what I know now that I've got my contractor's license. Half the work I do is deferred maintenance. That's the only way to prevent problems and ward off lawsuits."

He looked at his brother-in-law. "You're the lawyer, what do you think?"

Brad gave Patty a sympathetic wink. "Well, real estate's not my field. But it's true, lawsuits should be avoided."

She fidgeted with her napkin, not wanting to talk about her crisis or lawsuits. "May I have some salad, please?"

"Here, honey." Julia handed her the bowl. "By the way, how's your mother?"

Another one of Patty's favorite topics. "She's okay, you know, adjusting. Misses my dad."

"She must've been beside herself when she heard what happened to you." Cece's stepmom shook her head. "After everything she's been through these past few months."

Patty glanced at Cece. "Actually, my mother doesn't know. I haven't told her."

"Oh, I see." Julia pursed her lips. "I think she'd want to know, Patty. You're still her baby, no matter how old you are."

"My mother's not, well, not like that." She rubbed her left eye. "She's the tough one. My dad was the one we went to for comfort." Her voice cracked.

Phil, who was beside her, pulled her into his chest with both arms.

At first, she resisted, reluctant to accept his fatherly comfort, but then she gave in. Her grief, which she'd tried to suppress for months, burst to the surface, surprising her as much as everybody else.

She pushed her face into the older man's shirt, inhaling the scent of flannel and aftershave.

If only she could hug her own father one more time.

She hiccupped and straightened her back, letting Phil go. Everyone was looking at her with sympathetic eyes.

"So." Brad thumped the table. "How 'bout those Giants?"

To Patty's relief, the conversation turned to sports, weather, and wine.

She stood and cleared the table.

Cece joined her at the sink. “Sorry that got weird. You know my family—they mean well. They just don’t know when to shut up.”

She shook off her self-pity and rinsed the plates. “Isn’t that one of the things we love about them?”

Her friend leaned against the counter. “I suppose it is. I just hope they didn’t upset you.”

Patty shook her head. “The only thing that upset me was my reaction. God, I hate being emotional. It doesn’t suit me at all.”

“Yeah, I’d have to agree with that.”

The doorbell rang, and Cece looked at the clock. “You expecting anyone, honey?”

“Not that I’m aware of,” Brad said.

Julia headed to the front door. “I’ll see who it is.”

Patty put on the kettle for tea. She placed six mugs on a tray with honey, an assortment of teabags, spoons, and a plate of cookies.

The front door closed with a loud thud. Footsteps approached the kitchen.

“Look who’s here,” Cece’s stepmom said.

With tray in hand, Patty glanced over her shoulder.

Her hands let go of the tray, and it crashed to the floor, sending cookies and cups and broken dishes in every direction.

10

"Oh my God." Patty put a hand over her mouth.

"Patty," Julia said, "don't you want to introduce everyone to your sister?"

Cece squeezed her arm, as if it could calm her, and took control of the situation. "You must be Liza," she said in a gentle, warm voice.

A timid smile formed on Liza's pink lips. "I am."

Patty's mind raced with questions. She stared at her sister. Four months ago, her golden blonde hair had been down to her waist; now it barely touched her shoulders.

Liza bit her lower lip. "You're not happy to see me. I can tell."

Patty neither confirmed nor denied it. She was unable to grasp how her past and her present were colliding in the middle of Cece's kitchen. How did you know I was here?"

"I tracked your phone."

"My phone?" Her vision blurred.

"When you were home for the funeral. I authorized the app. Your password was easy to guess."

Cece raised an eyebrow. She'd told Patty a hundred times to mix up her passwords.

"So, you've been tracking me? Like the FBI or something?"

Liza's chest rose and fell. "No, well, not until—just a few times."

It gave Patty a chill to think of anyone watching her, even if it was only her little sister.

"Wait, how'd you get here?" she asked.

"I flew in an airplane."

"No, I mean here here, right *here*." Patty pointed at the floor. "Here to this house."

"Oh, I Ubered from the airport."

"What's an Uber?" Phil asked.

Julia shook her head. "I don't know."

"It's like a car service, Pop," Tom said. "Mostly for drunk college kids. They rarely come to Clearwater."

"That's right." Liza brightened. "My driver had never been here before. We got lost a bunch of times."

"Hold on," Patty said, trying not to overreact. Nothing about Liza tracking her phone, flying from Texas, and showing up at Cece's house made sense. "Why didn't you call me?"

Her little sister lowered her chin. "I was afraid you'd tell me not to come."

She probably would have, but she wasn't about to admit it in front of everyone. "My life is in complete chaos, Liza, I can't even…"

"Let's take a break." Cece angled herself between the sisters and put an arm around Liza. "Why don't you go wash up in Patty's room —it's right down the hall. Then come have something to eat, okay?

"Okay. Thank you." Her smile was that of a little girl.

Patty pulled Cece into the other room. "What're you doing?"

"What do you mean? I'm being nice to her." Her friend scowled. "And I don't understand what the problem is. You love

Liza, and now you're acting like she's going to steal your favorite shoes. Jesus, Patty, grow up!"

Cece's reprimand stung. Of course she loved Liza, but Clearwater was *her* safe haven, a separate place, a sanctuary. Nobody from her family belonged there, not even Liza.

Head hanging, she followed Cece back into the kitchen where Phil was putting on his jacket.

"I think I'll go home and watch the Giants game. You don't mind, do you, baby-girl?"

"No, Dad," Cece said. "Go ahead."

"I'll join you." Brad pushed back his chair.

"Me, too." Tom got in line behind his brother-in-law.

The three of them scurried out like nervous mice.

"Men. A few awkward moments and they head for the hills." Julia removed Noah from his highchair and carried him upstairs.

Patty rubbed her forehead. "Sorry I dropped the tray. I had no idea she was coming, and I have no idea why she's here. I'm kinda flipping out."

"You need to pull it together," Cece said. "Your sister's lovely, and she's welcome to be here."

She exhaled with a loud huff. "Fine."

"When Liza comes out we'll sit down and let her eat dinner without an interrogation. She'll probably tell us what's going on as soon as she's had a chance to relax."

"If you say so." Patty got out the broom to clean up the mess she'd made.

The last thing she wanted was to impose on her friend any more than she already had. And as sweet as Liza was, her surprise visit was sure to be an imposition on everyone.

"There you are," Cece said.

Patty dropped the broom with a clatter. Her sister was wearing her favorite UCLA sweatshirt. It was tight across the chest, and the sleeves barely covered her wrists.

"At least it's not my shoes." She mumbled under her breath.

"I hope you don't mind I borrowed your sweatshirt. I was cold."

"It's tight on you."

Cece coughed and bumped her shoulder.

"But it looks nice." Patty closed her mouth and pressed on her twitchy eye.

Liza sat at the table, her movements and gestures so familiar. Seeing her little sister reminded Patty of how she'd slipped out of the house in the midst of a panic attack without saying goodbye to her mother. The transgression still haunted her.

Julia returned to the kitchen and rested a hand on Liza's back. "Can I make you a plate, honey? You must be hungry."

"Yes, please." She picked at her blue nail polish. "I'm really sorry I interrupted your dinner."

"Nonsense." Julia filled a plate and served her. "We were finished anyway."

Liza smiled at the plate as if it were a surprise gift. "Thank you. This looks amazing."

The three women joined her at the table. Patty sensed she was nervous. Her little sister had never liked being the center of attention, but her surprise appearance made her just that.

"So," Cece said, breaking the silence. "What brings you to California?"

Liza chewed and swallowed. She patted the napkin to her lips. "I have a close friend from school who lives in San Francisco. I'm going to visit her."

"Oh, that's nice," Julia said, engaging as ever. "You're on summer break then?"

"Uh-huh." She sipped water. "Do you think I could have some wine? I'm twenty-one. I can show you my ID."

Patty bit back a laugh. Her sister had always been a goody-two-shoes.

"That's okay," Cece said, pouring with her left hand. "No ID necessary."

Patty motioned to Julia to keep the questions coming so she didn't have to ask them.

"And where do you and your friend go to school?"

"Princeton," Liza said quietly, as if she were embarrassed.

"Princeton?" Cece clunked her cast on the table. "I didn't know that."

"Liza's going to be a doctor," Patty said. "She's the smartest of the five of us. While I am the least smart."

"You're smart," Liza said. "Just in a different way."

Cece nodded. "That's true. You have an incredible eye for design."

"When we were little, Patty rearranged our room like once a month." She took a bite of steak. "This is delicious, by the way."

Julia continued her gentle questioning. "So, when are you meeting your friend in the city? Not tonight I hope. It's getting late."

"Well, we had to change the plan. Some things got messed up."

Patty's eye twitch started. She did not like changes in plans.

Liza continued eating, focused on the food. "My friend had a family emergency, which I didn't know until I landed. She's in Florida, I think. Anyway, she said I could go to her mom's apartment and the doorman would let me in, but then I just got the idea to find Patty instead." She raised her eyes. "I already knew you were up here."

Of course she did—she's been tracking me.

"What's your plan then?" Patty spoke lightly, trying to sound unconcerned. "I mean, until your friend gets back?"

Her sister's pale skin reddened. "Wouldn't mind being with you. It's only for a couple of days. And I saw a little motel close by where I could stay."

"Absolutely not," Julia said. "Between our two houses, we have several empty rooms."

"You'll stay here," Cece said.

"Really?" Liza beamed. "Can I share your room, Patty?"

"I don't think…"

"Of course, you can." Cece kicked her leg under the table. "It's a queen bed in there, plenty of room for two sisters."

Liza looked genuinely happy for the first time since she'd arrived.

"Oh boy, a slumber party." Patty stood and cleared the table.

After cleaning the kitchen, starting a load of laundry, and picking up a few toys, Patty was exhausted. She went to her room and found Liza sprawled across the bed, sound asleep. She had on kitty-cat pajama pants and a white T-shirt. Her heart softened. Her sister still had a smattering of freckles on her nose and cheeks. Fairy kisses, their father used to them.

Liza turned over, and the spell was broken.

Patty sat on the edge of the bed.

Did their mother know about Liza's spontaneous side trip to Clearwater? Did Maggie?

She took her phone into the kitchen and dialed her big sister's number. It didn't matter how late it was in Texas. Maggie hardly slept, anyway.

The phone rang once, twice… *What am I doing?* She dropped the phone, scrambled to pick it up, and disconnected the call.

She pressed her back against the wall and sank to the floor, relieved her moment of temporary insanity had passed. Alerting her older sister to her younger sister's sudden change in plans would lead to an interrogation, not only concerning Liza but Patty as well. As far as she knew, neither Maggie nor their mother were aware even *she* was in Clearwater. Best to lie low, float under the radar, and avoid family drama.

Besides, in a few days, Liza would be gone.

11

On the Wednesday after her sister's arrival in Clearwater, Patty started to get antsy. Liza's friend had postponed her return to San Francisco until Sunday.

A *couple of days* had turned into a week.

On the other hand, she couldn't discount how helpful it was to have Liza around. She was great with Noah, and her skill at French braiding was superior to Patty's. However, whenever she wasn't busy, her sister trailed after her, tagging along like a five-years-old.

When Patty was in the kitchen, so was Liza. When Patty went to Mariano's, so did Liza. When she bathed Noah, her sister sat on the bathroom floor and squirted water from the rubber ducky. She volunteered to do everything, as if she were clocking community service hours.

Patty stood on a step stool arranging jars of fancy lemon curd and raspberry confit into a beautiful display. A jar tipped and rolled off the edge. "Oh, crap!"

Liza caught it just before it hit the floor. "Why don't you let me do that? I'm taller."

"Okay. Thanks." She stepped down.

Tessa came out of the stock room just as they switched places. "Look at you, Liza," she said. "Thank goodness you're taller than your sister."

Her sister smiled, and she harrumphed.

"I have to go get Noah," Patty said. "Be back in about fifteen minutes."

"Okie-dokie." Tessa opened a jar of lemon curd, stuck a cookie in it, and offered it to Liza. "Here honey, have a taste. It's delicious."

Patty opened the door. "Okay, then, I'm going now. Bye." She waved at them, but they were too busy tasting lemon curd to notice.

She crossed the street and entered the park.

Beside the pavilion Rebecca had a crew of six dogs, including the cute brown mutt with the off-kilter nose.

"Hey, Rebecca," Patty said.

"Oh, hi, Patty." She jogged over with her canine charges. "Guess what, I met your sister yesterday. She's just the cutest!"

It was no surprise to hear Liza had even charmed the dog walker.

The brown dog sniffed Patty's leg and wagged his tail. He jumped, putting his front paws on her knees.

"Tipsy, no!" Rebecca pulled on the leash. She wore overalls again, but this time they were green. Instead of pigtails, she had a single braid down her back.

"I just saw this dog the other day, but I can't remember where," Patty said, although that wasn't true.

"Probably with me. I walk him all the time."

"No, he was with somebody else."

"He's the Hawk and Winters dog." Rebecca picked him up. "Maybe you saw him with Adam."

"Oh, that's right. Adam Hawk."

"You know Adam?"

"Not really," Patty said with a casual wave. "We've just crossed paths once or twice."

Rebecca scratched Tipsy under his chin. "The mysterious Adam Hawk. He's super hot, but kind of a jerk."

"Why do you say that?" She tried to sound only vaguely interested.

"He's always in a bad mood. Has been for like five years."

"Five years?" Patty laughed. "Even my bad moods don't last that long."

"It's because he has a broken heart."

Patty's interest skyrocketed. "Really?"

"Yeah, totally." Rebecca nodded, her eyes wide. "He was about to marry his high school sweetheart, but then something happened. Don't ask me what, because I don't know. But I can tell you it was a really bad break-up, and I mean super bad, like Romeo and Juliet bad."

"Romeo and Juliet didn't break-up. They died."

"Oh, yeah, right." Rebecca twisted her lips to the side. "I get my tragedies mixed up. Anyway, nobody talks about it because it started a feud between the two families. And that did happen in Romeo and Juliet."

Patty would've loved to hear more, but Cece was waiting for her. "Wish I could stay and chat, but I have to go get Noah." She bent and pet all the dogs, giving Tipsy a little extra attention.

"Hey, how long is Liza here?" Rebecca asked.

"She leaves on Friday for San Francisco."

"Is she coming back?"

"No." She responded more emphatically than intended. "She has to go home and get ready to go back to school."

"Oh," the dog walker said with a tiny pout. "Will you tell her to be sure to email me that recipe? It sounded so good."

"Recipe?"

The dogs pulled on the leash, and Rebecca jogged away, hollering over her shoulder. "She'll know. Bye, see ya!"

The girl was a treasure trove of information.

When Patty returned to the shop with Noah asleep in the stroller, Liza was sweeping up broken glass.

"What happened?"

"A customer dropped a jar, so I'm cleaning it up."

"Where's Tessa?" Patty asked.

"Running an errand."

"And she left you here alone? What if somebody came in and wanted to buy something or had questions about wines?"

Her sister tilted her head. "It's no big deal. She left five minutes ago, and she knew you were coming right back.

Patty didn't have an explanation for her snippiness. Only that Liza's presence had her on edge. Her sudden appearance, the change in plans with her friend—it was unsettling.

"Liza," she said in a measured tone. "Can I ask you a few questions?"

"Okay. What do you want to know?"

Patty leaned against the counter and ran her fingers across her lips. "For starters, why'd you cut off your hair?" She suspected it was an emotional reaction to their father's death. He'd loved Liza's long, blonde hair, the same hair their mother had had when they'd married.

"I got gum in it."

"Gum?"

Liza twirled her shoulder-length tresses. "Yeah, I was babysitting a few weeks ago, and one of the boys had gum in his mouth. Somehow it ended up in my hair."

"Oh." Patty chided herself for expecting some dramatic explanation. "I guess it'll grow back."

"I like it short," her sister said. "Don't you?"

"Actually, I do." She softened. Liza had always sought her approval. "It suits you."

"Thanks. So, what else?"

"Right, what else, oh yeah. I ran into Rebecca in the park, and she said you were sending her a recipe. What's that about?"

Her face lit up. "We met yesterday. She was walking a bunch of dogs, so I stopped to pet them. Anyway, we just started talking and somehow got onto baking. So I told her about my baking blog."

"Your baking blog?"

"Yeah. I've been doing it for a few months. I bake, take photos, post recipes. It's really fun, and you wouldn't believe how many followers I have."

"Wait a minute. How do you have time for baking and blogging when you're in school? You're pre-med. You hardly have time to breathe."

Liza tilted her head. "But I wasn't in school last semester. You knew that."

Patty nearly fell over. "No, I didn't."

"I told you when you were home for Daddy's funeral that I'd decided to take the semester off. You even said it was a good idea."

She had no recollection, not even an inkling. Could she have been so self-absorbed she hadn't heard her sister say she was taking a break from school?

"Geez, Liza, I don't remember anything about that." She rearranged Noah's blanket to give her hands something to do. The only thing she recalled about those two days was her desperation to leave. "I'm sorry."

"It's okay. You were, um, it was probably when you were busy with…" Liza finished sweeping the floor. She put the broom in the closet and picked up her backpack. "I guess I'll go now."

"Wait." Patty took a breath. How could she have been so indifferent to Liza's pain? "I should've listened better. It's just that, well, I was a basket case. Maggie was driving me crazy, taking charge of everything. Mom was being, well, you know how she is. And you were…" She stopped.

Liza was what? Patty had blocked it out, or at least had tried to. She hardly remembered being in the same room with her sister, unable to acknowledge anyone's suffering other than her own.

Her sister dragged a sleeve across her eyes. "I understand. You couldn't wait to leave, and I couldn't bear to. "

It wasn't an indictment or criticism, merely a statement. Not to mention, the disturbing truth.

12

Julia and Phil Camden's house bubbled over with noise and chatter.

"Dinner's ready, take your seats." Julia, the consummate hostess, welcomed everyone with equal measure, from beloved family members to stragglers like Patty—and Liza.

Patty took a seat beside Phil who sat in his spot at the head of the table.

Liza sat across from her, glancing in her direction every few seconds.

Ever since their conversation the other day, Patty sensed her sister could see inside her too deeply. Her astute assessment of Patty's reaction to their father's passing had touched a nerve. And her failure to hear Liza say she was taking a break from school was unforgivable.

What kind of big sister was she to have missed that?

Patty settled into the comfort and familiarity of Cece's parents' home and tried to quit beating herself up.

Liza had forgiven her, and as Cece had advised, Patty was moving forward and trying to do better.

She tore a slice of garlic bread in half and put a piece on her sister's plate.

Liza looked up. "Thanks," she said, her voice soft. She bit into the bread. "Julia, everything is delicious. I really appreciate being included in Sunday dinner."

"We're happy you're here," she said. "You'll be missed when you leave tomorrow."

A tiny twinge pinched Patty. She was relieved Liza was going, but a little sad, too. At least they'd cleared the air on a few things.

The conversation turned to San Francisco and the sights her sister should visit with her friend.

"If you get to Fisherman's Wharf," Tom said. "Go to Boudin's for the clam chowder bread bowl. It's the best sourdough in…"

A loud knock on the door, as if someone had kicked it, interrupted them.

Boomer, Julia's old boxer, growled and ran to the window.

"Another surprise visitor?" Phil winked at Liza.

"Not this time." Brad swung his legs over the bench and went to let his guest into the house. "Adam Hawk's delivering a case of wine. Phil, this is the one we're gonna split."

"Oh, good," Phil said. "I've been looking forward to it."

Patty forced down the food she'd just put in her mouth, gulped some water, and showed her teeth to Cece.

"What?"

"My teeth!" She opened her lips wider.

Cece poked at a spot. "Okay, you're fine."

The front door slammed.

Boomer barked, and the little brown dog ran into the kitchen. He circled the table as if he were chasing a rabbit.

"Tipsy, get back here!" Adam placed a box on the counter. "Sorry about that. I'll put him in the truck."

"Leave him be." Phil stood and greeted him. "He and Boomer can play."

Patty's stomach quivered.

Adam was a Greek god, all broad shoulders, taut muscles, strong hands.

Without taking her eyes off him, she whispered to Cece, "How is it you've never mentioned him before?"

"Never thought of it. I hardly even know him."

Tipsy put his front paws on Patty's leg. She lifted him into her lap and stroked his fur, anxious to see if Adam would remember her.

When Brad introduced her, Adam nodded without a glimmer of recognition.

He did, however, notice his dog sitting in her lap. His gray-blue eyes crinkled at the edges. "Look at that. Tipsy likes you."

She giggled too loudly. "Yeah, he, we—we've met before."

He angled his head. "Who? You and me, or you and my dog?" He smiled, and one side of his mouth tilted higher than the other.

Goosebumps rose on Patty's arms. The lopsided smile captivated her.

"Your dog." She almost said *both*, but she didn't want to draw attention to the fact their prior encounters had been unmemorable. She extended her hand. "I know Rebecca."

"I see." Adam grasped her hand tightly. His skin was warm. "Well, you know what they say, if you're okay by my dog, you're okay by me."

Do they say that?

Patty didn't move until Cece nudged her. She let go of his hand and went back to petting his dog.

"Why don't you join us?" Julia asked. "I made plenty."

"Thanks, but I just wanted to get these wines to Brad."

"Don't be ridiculous," Phil said. "Take a seat. Tom, go grab another bottle of wine."

"Hold on then," Adam said. "Allow me." He tore the box open, and his bicep bulged.

Patty's breath quickened.

"Half the case is a 2012 Cabernet. And the other half is my new Syrah. How about we open one of each? Brad, I'll replace them. These are on me."

"Won't argue with that," Brad said.

Just like that, Adam was in his element. He pulled the cork with one swift move, and the muscle on the back of his arm flexed.

Loud conversation created a hum in the room.

Patty rested her chin on her hand and watched him pour, mesmerized by his deep voice, as he talked about grapes and dirt and fermentation.

Cece scooted closer, breaking the trance she'd fallen into. "Stop staring."

She pulled away. "What're you talking about?"

Her friend gave her the you-know-darn-well-what-I'm-talking-about face.

"Patty?" Adam said.

She nearly sprang out of her seat. "Huh?"

He held up both bottles. "Want to try the Cab or the Syrah?"

She gazed into his eyes. "Both, actually."

"Atta girl. Woman after my own heart."

It wasn't only his heart she was after.

As Adam ate, he spoke about every aspect of evaluating wines by color, smell, and taste.

Patty leaned on her elbows, losing herself in one fantasy after another.

Adam and Patty and Tipsy walking in the park, picnicking on the lake, eating by candlelight, cuddling by a roaring fire in...

"Liza," Julia said. "Is something wrong?"

Patty's head snapped to the side, and her fantasies evaporated. "What happened?"

Liza held up her phone. “My friend just texted me. Something with her Grandma, so they’re staying in Florida.” She raised her shoulders as if it didn’t matter. “So I can’t go to San Francisco.”

“You still could go to the city,” Cece suggested. “You’re friendly with Rebecca. Maybe she can go with you one day this week.”

“I’m going on Tuesday,” Tom said. “Why don’t you come with me? You guys can explore while I meet with my supplier.”

“I don’t know.” Liza’s brow furrowed. “I think maybe I should just change my flight and go home tomorrow.”

Patty nodded. “I think that’s probably…”

“It’ll cost a fortune to move your flight,” Adam said.

She changed directions fast. “Adam’s right. It’s much too expensive to book a flight at the last minute.”

“But it means I’ll be staying with you until Thursday. That’s three extra nights.”

“Not a problem,” Cece said. “You’re the easiest house guest ever.” She winked at Patty.

Brad raised his glass. “To Liza hanging out a few more days. We’re happy to have you here.”

“You’re the nicest people in the whole world.” She smiled her sparkly smile, and threw her arms around Brad as if she’d known him forever.

Patty pressed the corner of her eye. Three more nights sharing her bed with Liza.

It was starting to get crowded.

13

Tessa handed Patty two corners of an embroidered tablecloth, and together they spread it over the round table in the cellar.

Technically, it wasn't a cellar; more of a hidden room off the storeroom. Recently decorated, it looked like an old-fashioned speakeasy, the walls lined with wine racks, old books, small antiques, and photos of the original Mariano brothers who immigrated from Italy at the turn of the century.

The room was used for tastings, small parties, and the occasional meeting. On the far side a narrow door opened onto the sidewalk. From the outside, if somebody didn't know to look for it, they'd pass right by it.

Tonight, Tessa had organized an informal girls' night out with Cece and Natalie.

Patty loved being included in their circle of friendship; it made her feel like she was part of the popular girl clique.

"What do you hear from Liza?" Tessa smoothed the tablecloth. "She enjoying San Francisco?"

"Definitely."

Her sister had texted a couple of photos from iconic destinations. Fisherman's Wharf, Lombard Street, and the Botanical Gardens in Golden Gate Park. Her message read,

HAVING THE BEST TIME!

They set they table together.

"When's she heading back to Texas?"

"Thursday." Patty's eye went twitchy. "I think."

"What's wrong with that eye?"

She rubbed it. Between her secret crush on Adam Hawk, Liza's change in plans, and no update from the landlord, her anxiety had spiked. "Nothing. It just twitches sometimes."

"I'd say more than just sometimes."

"It's a nervous tic from childhood. Much better than it used to be though."

"If you say so." Tessa climbed a wooden ladder that slid across the wall of wine racks. She pulled out two bottles of wine and tucked one under her arm.

"You're gonna drop that." Patty reached up. "Hand me one."

"I'm good," she said, coming down the ladder.

It looked precarious. Either the wine or the wine expert was likely to end up on the floor.

Tessa stepped off the bottom rung and placed the bottles on the corner table. With her back turned, she uncorked the bottles and decanted one of them. "Those need to breathe for a while, so don't touch."

"I promise I won't disturb them," Patty said.

A light tap-tap-tap on the secret door notified them of more guests.

Tessa peered through the viewer window, as if she had no idea who would've knocked. "What's the password?"

"Girls' night out," Cece whispered through the tiny window.

"That's right." She opened the skinny door.

Natalie and Cece, still dressed in black dance pants and tunics, entered, bringing in the delicious scent of freshly baked bread.

"I feel like I've just been admitted to a secret club," Cece said.

"I love what you've done in here, Tess." Natalie peered at an old picture on the wall. "It's got that hidden room vibe, like a Mafioso meeting place."

"Just the feel I was going for."

Cece put the box on the table and opened it, uncovering a loaf of crusty sourdough.

Patty's stomach rumbled. She'd spent the morning taking care of Noah and the entire afternoon at the shop. "Oh, yum." She broke off a piece. "I think I forgot to eat lunch today."

"You're a busy girl," Cece said. "Got a lot more on your plate than you're used to."

The understatement of all understatements.

Tessa clapped her hands. "Take seats." She put the decanter of red wine on the table.

"Shhh, don't bother the wine," Patty whispered. "It's still breathing."

"Don't make fun." Tessa gave her a stern look. "Have I not taught you the importance of serving wine correctly?"

"You absolutely have. Now, can we eat? I'm starving."

"Yes." Cece dished out the chopped salad with tongs.

"You've become an expert with your left hand," Tessa said, buttering a thick slice of bread.

"Yeah, I'm adjusting, but I'm sick of this cast. And Patty's sick of washing and braiding my hair."

"I'm not. I love doing your hair." She didn't mention how being needed gave her a sense of security, not to mention a lovely room in her friend's house.

Cece patted her knee. "Thank you, sweetie."

"A toast," Natalie said, raising her glass. "To my one-armed ballerina. Let's hope she gets her arm back soon."

They clinked glasses and drank.

Patty held the wine in her mouth. It was smooth, a hint of cherry.

"My God, Tess," Natalie said. "I don't believe it."

"What?"

Natalie laughed. She held her glass up. "This is Hawk and Winters."

Patty stopped chewing.

"No, it's not." Tessa raised her chin.

"Yeah, it is. It's the Pinot—I just had it last night."

"It's really good," Cece said. "Adam delivered a case of wines to Brad on Sunday. He even had dinner with us. Such a nice guy."

Patty tightened her jaw. She pictured the proverbial open can of worms.

"Really?" Tessa turned to Patty. "Were you there?"

She shrank. "Well, yeah, but it's not like *I* invited him."

"You," Natalie said, pointing at Tessa, "are as stubborn as they come."

"What're you talking about?" Cece asked.

Patty sat at attention and waited to hear the answer.

"Fine." Tessa gave Natalie a perturbed glance. "So it *is* Hawk and Winters. I just happened to have a few bottles on hand."

"It's absurd you don't carry his wines," Natalie said. "Can't you just let it go?"

"Let what go?" Cece asked. "I thought I knew everything around here."

Patty's head swiveled side to side like a spectator at a tennis match. Thankfully, Cece was asking all the right questions.

Tessa swirled her glass. "There's rift between our families. Ever since Adam broke up with my cousin, Kamila."

Patty choked. The bad break-up Rebecca had told her about

—now it made sense. So Tessa's problem with the Greek god wasn't about business. It was about family.

"Wait." Cece turned to Natalie. "I remember Kamila having a serious boyfriend in high school. Was that Adam Hawk?"

"Yep." Natalie nodded. "They were two years ahead of us. The golden couple. Everyone thought they'd get married. Then, about five years ago, it was over."

Cece shook her head. "How did I not know this?"

Tessa crossed her arms. "It happened when you were in Los Angeles. By the time you moved back here, it was old news."

Natalie scoffed. "Not for you, obviously. Geez, Tess, Kamila doesn't even live here anymore."

"I don't care. Kamila's a little sister to me. We were born on the exact same day, seven years apart, like kindred spirits. Our mothers are sisters, and the four of us were inseparable. The break-up changed everything. He practically ran her out of town."

Tessa swept her bangs out of her eyes and looked at Patty. "So, now you know why I won't carry his wines."

"Okay." She put up her hands, palms forward.

"Hold on a minute." Cece pointed at the decanter. "If you won't carry his wines, then why do you have this one?"

"I know why." Natalie slapped the table. "It's your brother's stash, isn't it? This is where he stores his wine ever since his basement flooded. And you know how excellent Adam's wines are, so you sneak a bottle from time to time. You replace it, of course, probably with something more expensive, and your brother is none the wiser."

Tessa pointed at Natalie. "You, my friend, should be a private investigator."

"This was not a difficult case." She waved away the matter. "Anyway, Tess, let it go. You're a fool not to sell his wines. I'll bet his Syrah will be winning awards at every festival in California."

Patty recalled Adam saying that same thing the day she was a fly on the wall and heard them arguing.

Tessa eyed Natalie. “Opinionated, are we?”

“We’re both businesswomen, and I’m giving you good advice. It’s time for you to move on.”

Tessa refilled her glass with Adam’s Pinot Noir. “Did it ever occur to you I don’t want to?”

The question dangled like a spider on a web. How intriguing. Maybe clinging to resentment and hurt feelings was easier than letting go.

“Well,” Natalie said, “you got me there. Let’s decant that second bottle and talk about something else.”

“Excellent idea.” Tessa perked up and refilled the decanter. “What’s on the agenda? Oh, I know, let’s talk about Liza. I adore that girl.”

Patty smiled thinly. “Everyone does.”

“Do I detect hint of jealousy?” Tessa asked.

“I’m not jealous of my little sister. It’s just that Clearwater is my—my refuge. And you’re *my* friends.”

Natalie laughed. “You sound like a teenager who has to drag her sister to the movie.”

“Whatever.” She fidgeted with her napkin. “I’m happy you all like Liza, I really am. And she *is* wonderful. And I’ll miss her when she goes home in two days.”

“You know,” Cece said. “She could stay longer.”

Patty nearly knocked over her wine. “I don’t think so.”

“Why not? She loves it here, she’s great with Noah, and she’s helpful beyond belief.”

“That’s true.” Tessa lifted her wine glass.

“And,” Cece said, “it gives you more time to make things right. To do better.”

Patty’s eye twitched. It was her turn on the hot seat.

“I agree,” Tessa said. “There’s some lingering tension between the two of you.”

Natalie buttered a piece of bread. "Take it from me, Patty. I'm an only child and would've loved a little sister. Siblings are a blessing."

Patty's eyes stung. Countless times her father had said just that—"*your brothers and sisters are a great blessing, Patty-cakes, don't push them away.*"

"You don't understand how complicated Liza is. She's too smart for her own good." She rubbed her left eye.

Liza had the ability to see things in her she didn't see in herself. It was weird—and kind of creepy.

"I have no idea what that means." Tessa fluttered her long lashes. "But I do know you're lucky to have a sister like Liza."

She looked to her best friend for support.

"Don't look at me. It was my idea."

Patty gripped the edge of the table. "You know my life is crazy, don't you? I'm in debt, my apartment is condemned, and my mother's pretty much not speaking to me." She stopped before adding, *And I have a crush on Adam Hawk who was, or still is, in love with Tessa's cousin.* "And let me tell you this. There's something going on with Liza, something she won't tell even me."

"Well," Cece said, "you're the big sister. If there's something going on, it's your job to figure out what it is."

By the time Patty got into bed, anxiety was oozing out her pores.

Her three friends had convinced her to invite Liza to stay another week.

"Damn!" She threw off the covers. It was midnight, and her little sister still wasn't back.

How could Tom have kept them out so late? What if they'd gotten into trouble or had an accident?

For the umpteenth time, she checked her cell for messages.

She was tempted to wake up Cece. If Patty was going to worry about Liza, then she ought to be worrying right along with her. After all, it was her brother who'd taken Liza into the city.

At the sound of Tom's truck rumbling up the driveway, she flew back into bed.

Liza entered on tip-toes, went straight into the bathroom, and closed the door without a sound.

Patty listened to her sister's familiar bedtime bathroom process. She could even hear the sound of her flossing her teeth.

When Liza was five, they both went to the dentist. At the time, she was thirteen with a mouthful of braces and swollen gums.

The dentist had scolded her in front of a very concerned little Liza for not flossing. From then on, until the day Patty left for college, her sister reminded her to floss.

The bathroom door opened, and the light went out.

Liza got into bed, barely jiggling the mattress, and pulled the blanket up.

Patty pretended to be sound asleep. A few seconds later, her sister scooted closer. Then closer again, just like she used to when she was a little girl.

She could smell her lavender hand cream and minty toothpaste.

14

Liza jumped up from the table, sloshing coffee. "Really? You mean it? You want me to stay longer?"

Patty mopped up the spill. "It was Cece's idea."

Her sister hugged both of them. "I'm so excited. And I'll watch Noah whenever you want me to."

"Thank you, Liza, but that's not why we invited you stay. We all love having you here. Right, Patty?"

"Uh-huh," she said with false enthusiasm.

"I need to call Mom and tell her she doesn't have to pick me up tomorrow. And then I'll change my flight to next week. Oh! I'm so excited." She practically skipped out of the kitchen.

"Look how happy she is," Cece said. "It's so cute. Reminds me of you when we first met."

She rubbed Patty's head, messing up her hair.

Even Cece was starting to annoy her.

Patty cut a slice of smoked gouda and topped it with a spicy plum and pepper chutney from a new supplier.

Tessa had recognized her discerning palate and keen sense of smell, so she made her the official taster. If Patty liked something, they ordered it.

Her mouth was full when Rebecca came into the shop.

"Hey, Patty!" She had Adam Hawk's dog with her. "What're you eating?"

"A new chutney." She put a dollop on a cracker. "Try it."

The dog walker popped it into her mouth. "Yum. My mom would love this. How much?"

"We don't carry it yet, but I'm going to order some. We'll have it next week."

"Boy," Rebecca said, putting Tipsy down. "You're really running this place, aren't you?"

"Not really," she said, although she was working hard. And for the first time in years, she loved what she was doing. "So, I heard you and Liza had a great time in the city yesterday."

"We sure did! And Cece's brother is totally nice. Do you know if he's single? Do you think he's too old for me?"

Patty rolled her eyes. "Yes he's single, and yes he's too old for you."

"Too bad. Anyway, is Liza here?"

"Not at the moment." She opened another new chutney.

"Okay, I'll text her then. Now that she's staying longer, she's going to teach me how to make the cupcakes we talked about yesterday."

"Uh-huh." Patty only half-listened. She was preoccupied with a new flavor—mango, tomato, jalapeno. Her taste-buds danced with delight.

"Can you do me a favor?" Rebecca asked.

"Sure." She read the ingredients on the side of the jar. There was a hint of spice that intrigued her.

"Can you watch Tipsy for a couple minutes?"

"What?" Patty snapped to attention. "No."

"No?"

The request had caught her off guard. "I can't. I've got orders to fill."

"You don't need to do anything. He'll just go to sleep in the corner until Adam comes to pick him up."

She glanced at the brown mutt who was sniffing around the counters and shelves, his nails clicking on the hardwood floor. "I really can't have a dog in the shop."

"Buttercup's allowed in the shop."

"Buttercup belongs to Tessa."

"Well, whatever. I'll just tie him up outside." She picked Tipsy up and nuzzled him. "You'll wait outside for your daddy, okay?"

"You're leaving him outside? What if he gets stolen?"

Rebecca laughed. "You big city people, always worrying about the silliest things." She left with a carefree wave.

Patty put lids on the chutney jars and went to work on a gift basket. She glanced outside every few seconds.

Tipsy, his leash tied to the bench next to the door, wagged his tail and greeted every person walking by.

Patty tore a piece of cellophane from the roll, wrapped it around the basket, and secured it with a ribbon of raffia and dry flowers. She set the basket on the counter beside the register, and looked out the window.

Tipsy, his hind legs on the bench and his front paws on the window ledge, was looking through the glass. He barked.

"You're just too cute." She filled a dish with water and brought it outside. She crouched on her heels and stroked Tipsy while he drank.

"Hey there."

She looked up. Adam Hawk stood over her.

Patty tried to stand but lost her balance and fell on her behind. "Ouch!" She wanted to sink into the sidewalk. Her palms burned, her tailbone ached, and her face burned like fire.

Falling in front of the Greek god—*how could she?*

"You okay?" He took her by the wrist and pulled her to her feet.

"Oh, sure." She brushed her hands on her pants, refusing to meet his gaze.

"Thanks for giving Tipsy water."

"Um, yeah, water. He looked, uh, uh…" What was wrong with her? She never bumbled around men, but then she'd never been around a man like Adam Hawk.

"Thirsty?"

"Right, thirsty." Patty straightened her shoulders and willed herself to quit acting like a dimwit.

She wanted to continue the conversation but had no idea what to say. The only time she'd ever seen him animated was when he talked about wine.

Yes, wine.

"Oh, Adam, would you mind helping me? I need to, um, to select a bottle of wine for a gift basket. I could use your advice." Her clever ploy sent her confidence soaring.

"I don't think that—"

"Tessa's gone for the day."

He gave her quizzical look. Obviously, he didn't know she knew about the feud.

Patty tried to untangle her words. "And she's the one who decides on the wines for the gifts, so I'm kind of at a loss. You'd be doing me a big favor."

"Well, it was nice of you to give Tipsy a dish of water." His lopsided grin appeared. "So I guess it's the least I can do."

Patty's mouth went dry. Was he flirting with her?

Adam and Tipsy followed her inside.

She felt like a teenager sneaking a boy into the basement.

"What's the gift for? A birthday or something?"

"Actually, an anniversary." She made everything up as she went along. "The customer asked for something romantic, like for a picnic by the lake."

"Romantic, huh?" He twisted his mouth to the side and perused the wines on display. "You know, most people think champagne is the most romantic wine."

"Champagne is wine?" Patty asked absently.

Oh, what a stupid question!

"It is," he said, as if the question wasn't stupid at all. He took a bottle off the shelf, read the label, put it back. "But in my view, a silky Pinot Noir is the most seductive choice."

Pinot Noir, the wine Tessa had served last night.

Oh, what a perfect description—*silky, seductive.*

Patty could listen to him talk forever.

Adam continued his examination of the wines, his expression changing like a turning kaleidoscope. Some wines were met with a frown, some with a nod of the head, and some with a dropped jaw. He held a bottle in both hands. "My God. She never ceases to amaze me."

"What?"

"Can you ring this up for me?" He handed her a French Pinot Noir.

"Okay." Patty felt invisible, as if he and the wines were all alone.

The wine cost sixty dollars—not cheap, but not the most expensive either.

Adam paid with cash. His money was neatly folded and secured with a money-clip, the bills crisp and unwrinkled.

It reminded her of the way her father had kept his money.

Patty started to place the wine in a bag.

"Not yet." He took the bottle from her and uncorked it.

"Do you want a decanter?" she asked

Adam looked up, as if he'd forgotten she was there. "Not for this one." He removed two wine glasses from the rack above his head and poured a small amount into each glass. He swirled it, looked at in the light, and stuck his nose into the glass. Then he sipped, held the wine in his mouth, and swallowed. The sound he made was one of pure pleasure.

She copied everything he did. "Oh!" She choked on the wine. It tasted awful.

The Greek god laughed. "I'm sorry, I should've warned you. French Pinots are hard to get used to. They're different from ours here in California."

Patty smacked her lips and ate a cracker to soothe her mouth. "I liked the Pinot we had last night much better."

"Really?" His interest in her shot up like a rocket. "What did you drink last night?" His eyes shined with curiosity.

She tripped all over herself. "I—I don't remember." Her voice squeaked. "Something Tessa selected."

"Hmmm, I'll bet it was BenderSmith. Their Pinots are very good." He pushed the cork into the bottle and placed it in the bag. "Anyway, as for your gift basket, you can't go wrong with a Sonoma Pinot priced at twenty or more." Adam pulled food items from the shelves—a small tin of caviar, crackers, olives, spicy onion relish.

"You want a mix of sweet and savory. Put in a piece of gouda or even sharp cheddar, a salami, a bag of Marcona almonds. The smoked paprika ones are my favorite." He set everything on the counter and nodded, as if approving his selection. "A package of those lavender shortbread cookies, some dark chocolate, and you're good to go."

Patty had fallen into a daze listening to him. "Thank you." Her voice was breathy.

"Happy I could help," he said. "Ready, Tips?"

Tipsy jumped up and wagged his tail.

She didn't want him to leave. "How'd you choose the name 'Tipsy'?" she asked, hoping to start another conversation.

Adam scooped up his dog and tucked him under his arm like a football. "Well, it's kind of a funny story. I was going through a bad time, and some friends took me out to cheer me up. Needless to say, I drank too much. When I woke in the morning, this little guy was in my bed, and I had no idea where he'd come from. I'm pretty sure I found him wandering on a road somewhere. Although, he might've found me that way. I suppose we found each other."

"That's so sweet."

One corner of his mouth curved up. "Yeah." He kissed his dog's head.

She scratched Tipsy's ears. "So, how long have you had him?"

"About five years." He clipped the dog's leash to his collar. "It was June. So, yeah, exactly five years ago."

Ah, right, the big break-up.

Her attraction to him ticked up another notch. What was it about sensitive men who loved dogs?

He put Tipsy down and opened the door. "Hey, Patty." Adam rocked on his heels. "You ever need help again, you know, with wine or whatever, let me know."

Her dry lips parted. "Uh, okay."

The moment he was out of sight, Patty did the happy dance.

Tessa noticed the Pinot Noir was gone the next morning. "That's odd," she said. "I put a French Pinot up here the other day. Did you move it?"

"Oh, um, someone bought it yesterday." Patty focused on the pepper jack cheese she was slicing.

"You're kidding. One of our regulars?"

"I don't think so."

"Man or woman?"

Why did it matter? "A man."

"Did he say anything about it?"

Tessa's persistence intrigued her.

Patty continued slicing cheese. “He was impressed to have found it. Why?”

“Because it had to be a collector—or maybe a sommelier.” She rearranged some bottles. “I’d love to find out who it was. I don’t know many people who appreciate French Pinot Noirs.”

Patty wrapped the cheese and put it in the cooler. She wondered how long it would take Tessa to discover how much she admired the man she couldn’t stand.

15

Orders for Father's Day gift baskets poured into Mariano's. Patty's fingertips were raw from tying ribbons and raffia.

On Friday afternoon, they received a slew of last-minute orders. Patty set up an assembly line on a table in the back. She filled the baskets with crinkle paper, placed a bottle of wine in the center, and arranged food items around it, keeping in mind Adam's instructions to mix savory and sweet.

"You do a beautiful job," Tessa said, pulling a long piece of ribbon from the spool.

"Thanks." She wanted Tessa to be happy with her work, even if it was just temporary. "I like doing this kind of thing. I have an eye for balance."

They exchanged uneasy smiles.

"You look like you to have something to say."

Tessa cleared her throat. "Well, I'm just wondering how much longer you'll be here."

The question was reasonable, but Patty couldn't answer it. She had more loose ends than an old sweater. Her duplex was uninhabitable, and she hadn't spoken to her supervisor at Pottery Barn in weeks.

"I'm not really sure. Liza's going home soon, then Cece will probably get her cast removed, so after that, I guess." She stuffed a handful of paper into a basket.

"I'm just thinking about the schedule," Tessa said, swapping out the wine in one of the baskets. "It's almost July, and summer's my busiest time of year. So I have to plan ahead. You do understand, don't you?"

"Of course." She tried to control her eye without touching it. Their agreement had been ambiguous from the start, but the money she earned working at the shop was keeping her afloat. If Patty were let go now, she'd sink like a brick. "Let me talk to…"

The bells jingled, and a woman entered. She had dark wavy hair, red fingernails, and what looked like a fancy designer handbag.

Tessa moved toward her. "Sophia, you're early."

"Oh, I know. I just had my nails done, so I was already in town. Finish whatever you're doing; I'll wait in the cellar."

The woman left through the storeroom as if she'd been to the cellar many times before.

Why hadn't Tessa introduced them? She always introduced Patty to her friends, usually with high praise.

"Listen. We'll talk more later. Why don't you go to Nutmeg's and get a coffee? Put it on my account."

"Okay." Patty kept her voice steady. "Do you want anything?"

"No, I'm fine." Tessa waved a hand and disappeared through the swinging door.

Patty felt like a cat being swept out with a broom.

Outside, the sun sparkled on the sidewalk. She sat on a bench in front of the candy store and called her landlord. For the last week, her calls and texts had gone unanswered. It was time to take action.

The phone rang only once before the auto-message picked up.

She sighed and waited for the beep. "Hey, it's Patty Sullivan again. I hope the work on my ceiling is coming along. I uh, well, it's been over a month since I was locked out of my apartment, and, um, I need to…" Her voice cracked. "I need to know when I can go home. Okay, call me back. Thanks—bye."

Patty folded and unfolded her hands. Between her landlord ignoring her calls and Tessa shooing her out the door, she sensed trouble coming her way.

With adrenaline pumping through her system, she jogged toward Nutmeg's.

As she approached the corner, another shot of adrenaline hit her bloodstream. "Oh my God."

Adam Hawk sat at one of the outside tables, his head down as if reading something.

At least she had on cute jeans and a green shirt that brought out the color in her golden-green eyes.

She hid behind a lamppost, finger combed her hair, then crossed the street with nonchalance. She wanted to appear surprised when their eyes met. *He'd say hello, she'd respond with an engaging smile, and say something witty like…*

"Oh!" Her heel caught the curb. She lurched forward, stumbled, and smacked the sidewalk with her left hip.

She prayed Adam hadn't seen her, but before she even lifted her head, he was crouching beside her.

"Man, you went down hard."

Patty got to her knees. "Yeah, I did." Her hip throbbed.

"Lemme help you," he said, taking both her arms in his strong hands. "This is the second time you've fallen in front of me."

And the second time she wanted to be swallowed by cement. But at least he remembered. "I'm not usually so clumsy."

Just as she regained some composure, a woman with long,

very straight dark hair came out of Nutmeg's. She placed two drinks on the table.

"What's going on?" The woman wore white jeans frayed at the ankle, a light blue shirt, and silver sandals. Her toenails were red and sparkly. She looked like she'd just stepped out of a fashion Pinterest page.

"Nothing," Adam said. "Just helping out a friend."

A friend.

Okay, at least they were *friends*, now.

It took a little of the sting out of her embarrassment.

"Do you want to sit for a minute?" Adam asked.

"Oh, no, I can't. I'm just getting a latte. I hope Trevor's working. He makes the best lattes, and I always try and come when he's the barista." She covered her lips. *Stop rambling!*

"You might need a shot of whiskey in that latte." He smiled, one corner of his mouth higher than the other.

The woman walked over. "You're Patty, aren't you?"

Her brow went up. "Um, yes."

"I'm Kamila, Tessa's cousin."

Blood drained from her face. She masked her shock and extended a hand. "Hi. I love your—your toes." Patty cringed.

"Thank you." Kamila's smile, all shiny white teeth with dimples on both sides, unnerved her.

She had the same wide-set brown eyes as Tessa, with even thicker lashes.

"I have to go," Patty said.

"What about your latte?"

"Oh, right, um, well…" Her insides churned. "Changed my mind. I got to get back to the shop. Tessa's waiting for me. Gotta make more Father's Day baskets."

Kamila put a hand on her arm. "I saw your beautiful baskets. You're quite creative, especially the epicurean variety of flavors."

Patty blinked. Was it a compliment? Or did Kamila know Adam had advised her on how to pair sweet and savory?

"I look forward to learning from you." Her smile shone even brighter.

"Excuse me?"

"I probably shouldn't have said anything yet, but I'm excited about it. I've always wanted to work with Tessa."

"You're going to work at Mariano's?" Her ex-boyfriend crossed his arms. "Don't you think that's a…"

"It'll be fine, Adam. Now, why don't we get back to our coffee? See you soon, Patty." Kamila lifted her sweetheart chin.

Patty resisted the urge to bolt. It was the second time she'd been dismissed in less than thirty minutes. "Right. Okay, bye." She managed a feeble smile.

Adam put a hand on her back. "You sure you're okay? I mean, that was quite the fall."

His touch set her skin on fire. "Oh, sure, I'm sure sure sure." *Just shut up!*

She stepped off the curb and walked with slow, deliberate steps to hide her jitters. As soon as she was a block away, Patty kicked off her sandals and ran to the shop.

Tessa looked up when she threw open the door.

"What's the matter?" She sliced through the tape on a box with a pocket knife. "I thought you were getting coffee."

"I got distracted." Patty pushed Adam out of her mind. "Guess what. I met your cousin."

"Kamila?"

"Uh-huh. She was there with Adam Hawk."

That got Tessa's attention. "Really? Well, I suppose they have things to discuss."

Patty shifted. Her hip ached, and her hands shook. "Kamila said something about coming to work here. Kinda caught me off guard."

"I understand." Tessa pursed her lips. "It's all happened very fast. I was about to bring up the subject when Sophia arrived."

"Sophia?"

"The woman who came in earlier. That was my aunt, Kamila's mother. I should've introduced you, but she's kind of difficult. Controlling, actually. To be honest, she sometimes annoys me."

"Oh." Patty took it all in. One more Mariano woman to keep track of.

"She's very sensitive about Kamila. Wants to help her get settled after, you know, being gone five years. It's a transition time."

"So, you *are* hiring her?" She reminded herself that business decisions were just that—business—and not to be taken personally.

"It looks that way, and it'll be fine. You can show her the ropes. And if the two of you overlap for a while, that's okay. I can afford to pay you both."

Patty breathed easier. At least she wouldn't be thrown out before her apartment was repaired and she could go home. "Okay. I didn't mean to overreact, I was just surprised."

"I get it." Tessa moved toward the Father's Day basket work station. "Now let's finish unpacking this wine and get back to making baskets. By the way, I love your selection of items. You've developed a real aptitude for pairings."

"I'm glad you think so."

"Well, you are learning from the master."

"Very true." Patty nodded, avoiding eye-contact, and faked an easy-going smile.

Two masters.

16

Early on Father's Day morning, Patty woke up with a headache. Or maybe a stomach ache. Or maybe she had a fever.

It didn't matter.

The day she'd been dreading was upon her.

Liza had moved into an upstairs bedroom, so Patty had the bed to herself again. She rolled onto her stomach, pushed her face into the soft pillow, and went back to sleep.

At noon, she opened her eyes to bright sunlight peeking through the side of the blind.

Patty groaned. Her head still ached, her feet hurt, and her fingertips were raw from tying so many ribbons.

She dragged herself out of bed and into the shower. As the hot water soaked her head and ran down her body, she contemplated the next few weeks.

Once Cece got her cast off, she'd leave Clearwater. By then, her sister would be long gone, Tessa would have Kamila in place, and Patty could head back to LA and get her life in order.

The biggest concern was whether or not her apartment would

be ready. If Patty went home before the repairs were complete, her options weren't pleasant.

She had no extra money, so coming up with first and last month's rent for a new place was impossible. Because she was on a month-to-month lease, the owner of the duplex had no obligation to house her.

A horrible thought made her choke. What if she had to move back to Texas? Dread washed over her, and she trembled, despite the warm water sluicing down her body.

Patty got out of the shower and toweled her hair. She put on black sweat pants, a black shirt, and even black socks. It suited her mood.

The smell of chocolate lured her into the kitchen.

Liza, wearing her UCLA sweatshirt, stood at the island running a sharp knife horizontally through a round chocolate cake. With intense concentration, her sister lifted a layer and placed it on a plate, unaware she was being observed.

Her blonde hair was pulled back in a short ponytail, a few loose strands hanging in her face. For a brief moment, Patty caught a glimpse of the little girl her sister used to be.

"You're wearing my sweatshirt again."

Liza jumped. "Oh, hi." Her voice was cheery. "Yeah, it's small on me, but I love it. I saved you a cup of coffee." She pointed to a mug on the counter.

"Thanks." She put it in the microwave. "Where's everyone?"

"At Julia and Phil's for Father's Day brunch."

"Oh, yeah, I forgot."

She and Liza had been invited, but they'd both declined.

"What're you baking?"

"Chocolate-whiskey cake. I told Cece I'd be in charge of dessert for the barbecue tonight."

Patty rubbed her chest. "You're sticking around for the barbeque?"

"Yeah, aren't you?"

"No. This isn't a happy day for us, Liza."

Her sister picked up a dishtowel and wiped her hands. "It isn't about *us*."

The microwave pinged. She got her coffee, burning her hand. "It's our first Father's Day with no father," she said, raising her voice. "I hardly think we should go to a party."

Liza pursed her lips. "Do you think Daddy would want us to be sad? I think he'd want us to celebrate the day. And he'd want us to do the right thing."

"Really? And what's the right thing he'd want us to do?"

Her sister's expression was a mix of surprise and disapproval. "Cece wants you here, Patty. And after everything she's done for you, the least you can do is be here to help."

The dig was sharp, especially coming from Liza.

Patty wanted to walk out and avoid her sister's judgement, but she steeled herself and stayed.

Liza had as much right to be short-tempered as she did.

"Did you know," her sister took a weary breath. "I've been baking for years?"

Patty closed her eyes. She knew nothing about the baking or any other hobbies her sister had. There were so many things about Liza she didn't know or understand.

"I didn't."

"I started when you left home." She drizzled melted chocolate over the whipping cream and folded it in with a rubber spatula. "I was only ten, and the person I loved most in the world had left."

Patty sat on a stool. Her sister's remark was unfair. "I went to college, Liza. That's what I was supposed to do."

"I know. But you weren't supposed to forget me."

Forget Liza? Is that really what she thought?

"I never forgot you."

"It felt like you did." Tears rolled down her cheeks. She brushed them away with the back of her hand.

Patty's chest ached. How many times had Liza left messages on the answering machine? How many times had Cece said, "*Your little sister called, call her back.*"?

How many times had she reached for the phone to call then been distracted or changed her mind, or figured it was too late and she'd call tomorrow?

The conversation was long overdo.

She'd skirted it for years, but now, with Liza all grown up and astonishingly mature, the truth was unavoidable.

Patty had deserted her little sister.

She still could not face the guilt.

"Do we have to do this now? Today of all days?"

Liza sighed. "No. You can put off talking about our relationship as long as you want. I get it."

She snapped at her. "You get what?"

Her sister put down the spatula. "I get you can't handle the hard stuff. You couldn't deal with being home after the funeral, so you left. And you couldn't deal with me being a clingy, annoying little sister, so you cut me out of your life." Liza turned away.

It'd been over a decade since she'd graduated high school and took off, leaving her ten-year-old sister alone with a distracted father trying to hold onto his business and a mother tired of mothering.

She had no response, other than to defend the indefensible. "You don't know what it was like for me, the black sheep of the family. Never as smart, never as pretty, always the one in trouble." Patty recalled every teacher in school shaking their heads in disbelief when they discovered she was a Sullivan.

They told her she looked different; some even expressed their disappointment she wasn't gifted like her siblings.

Maggie and the boys were perfect, so she did everything in her power to be the opposite of that.

"All of you are beautiful and smart, just like Mom, and I'm

the one stuck with some bizarre genetic mutation that gave me bright red hair and a low IQ." As the words came out, even she could hear how crazy she sounded.

"You suffered because you had red hair?" Liza's voice shook. "And you're not as smart as I am? Well, be grateful for that. I'm so smart, I ended up on the other side of the country, away from everyone I love, all because Mom had to have one of her children get a degree from Princeton." Her blue eyes flashed. "I never wanted to go there. And I hate snow!"

She'd never seen her sister like this. She was always so sweet and gentle, wanting to please everyone, especially Patty. Now Liza's pent up grief and anger was erupting.

It was time for her to admit the truth, to accept the blame. She was the older sister; she should've done better.

She touched Liza's arm. "I don't really understand why you wanted to see me, why you want to spend all this time with me. I mean, I've been a crappy sister for a long time. You should hate me. I would if I were you."

She shook her head. "I could never hate you. You were the only one who wanted me."

Her dry lips parted. "What d'you mean?"

"It doesn't take a genius IQ to know I was a mistake."

Telling Liza she was wrong would be a lie.

Patty still remembered her mother crying for weeks after finding out she was pregnant at the age of forty.

Perhaps honesty was the best policy when it came to accidental babies.

"You're right about both. You were a surprise baby, and I did want you. And in the spirit of true confessions, I wanted you to be like me. When you were born, you were so tiny. You even had red hair for a while. And you hardly talked until you were three. Then when you were five, your hair turned blonde, you grew so big I couldn't even pick you up, and you started reading the newspaper."

"The newspaper?"

She nodded. "Yep. Daddy thought it was adorable. Mom said you were a genius. And I just figured you were turning into Maggie."

"But I'm nothing like Maggie."

"You're definitely not." Patty brushed some hair out of her sister's eyes. "And I have news for you. You weren't the only accident. *I* was one, too."

Her eyes widened. "You were?"

"I was." Patty nodded. "I didn't figure it out like you did though. Maggie told me."

"She *told* you? When? And why?"

"When I was about seven. We got into a big fight 'cause I used her new lipstick to paint a picture. I'd never seen her so furious, and she just blurted it out. '*Mom and Dad only wanted three babies. You never should've been born'.*"

"That's terrible. Even for Maggie."

"Well, to be honest, pissing off our big sister was my favorite activity. Anyway, I tattled, she got grounded, and Daddy gave me lots of extra attention." Patty smiled at the memory, her father saying, '*surprise babies are gifts from God.'*

"That sounds like him." She went back to whipping cream.

"Hey." Patty nudged her. "Just because we weren't wanted doesn't mean we weren't loved."

Her sister looked at her with a wistful smile. "We were loved, especially by Daddy, weren't we?"

"Definitely."

Liza handed her the spatula and dipped another one into the mixture. "To Daddy," she said.

"To Daddy," Patty echoed.

They toasted their father with spatulas coated in chocolate whipped cream.

17

As Liza had predicted, Cece was delighted to have them at the Father's Day barbeque.

Patty moved through the event in a daze, thinking about the last time she'd seen her father and wishing she could change the past. She watched Cece and Tom tend to Phil, the patriarch, and smiled at the sight of Brad showing off Noah, as if his son's existence still amazed him.

Liza presented her cake after dinner, claiming she and Patty had made it together.

She was appreciative to be given some credit, even though all she did was clean up the mess.

The cake was a work of art—three layers of double chocolate whiskey cake with cream filling between each and topped with a mound of white and dark chocolate curls.

On Monday morning, Patty woke at sunrise. She'd had bad dreams all night, and her bruised hip bothered her every time she rolled over.

She shuffled into the kitchen in her pajamas.

Brad, wearing a suit and tie, was drinking coffee and reading the sports page. "What are you doing up so early?"

"I haven't been sleeping so well." She took a mug from the cabinet and filled it with coffee and cream.

"Still no news from your landlord?"

"Nope."

He stood, folded the paper, and put his breakfast dishes in the sink. "One of my partners deals with landlords all the time. Want me to run your situation by her?"

Patty hated to involve Brad in her troubles. She'd already brought enough chaos into his house. "No thanks. I gotta figure it out myself."

He patted her on the back. "As you wish."

As I wish. I wish I knew what to wish.

After Brad left, she showered and dressed.

Like clockwork, Noah called for *Titi* at 7:30 on the nose, his muffled voice coming through the monitor.

She'd been his morning person for nearly six weeks, so he called for her now instead of Cece. Her heart did a little pitter-patter every time she heard him call her name.

Still, it was mind-boggling how much care a toddler needed. With Cece incapacitated, a team of people had stepped in. Between Patty, Julia, Liza, and a trio of Cece's older ballet students, Noah had a virtual harem of woman looking after him.

"G'morning, big boy." She opened the door to his room.

He stood at the rail grinning, his chin wet with drool. "Ti-ti!"

Patty lifted him and blew a raspberry on his cheek, making him squeal with delight. She changed his diaper and dressed him in denim overalls.

"Good morning," Cece said, coming into the room.

"Mama!" Noah extended his pudgy hands to his mother.

"It's killing me I can't pick him up."

Patty finished snapping the snaps between his chubby legs. She pointed to the glider. "Sit."

Patty put the baby in his mother's lap.

Cece nuzzled his neck and kissed his face. "Hey, thanks for being with us last night. I know it wasn't easy for you."

"It was fine," Patty said. She folded a blanket and hung it on the side of the crib. "No big deal."

"Yes it was. It was a very big deal."

"Okay, yeah, it was hard. And I wouldn't have even been there if Liza hadn't talked me into it. As usual, my sister was right." She sighed. "Getting past this first Father's Day was just a hurdle we had to get over."

"How'd your mom handle it?"

Patty averted her eyes.

"You didn't call her?"

"I forgot." The truth was she didn't want to. Avoidance was her comfort zone. But it had been her mother's first Father's Day without her husband. "I should've called her, huh?"

Cece let Noah wriggle off her lap. She stood. "You're almost thirty-years-old, Patty. I don't need to tell you what the right thing to do is."

She flinched. Few things hurt more than Cece's disapproval.

At nine-fifteen, after getting Cece and Noah dressed and fed, Patty left for work.

A steady stream of customers came into the shop, and orders were being placed by phone and online. They could use an extra set of hands, even if those hands belonged to Kamila.

Working side by side with Tessa's cousin, who happened to be the ex-girlfriend of the guy she had a crush on, would be interesting at the very least.

Patty placed a tin of smoked oysters on a new window

display she called, *Picnic by the Lake*—an assortment of food inspired by the romantic picnic basket Adam had put together.

An image of him and Kamila having a romantic dinner on a blanket by the water entered her mind. They definitely were a beautiful pair.

She shook the illusion out of her mind and told herself to forget Adam Hawk. Kamila or no Kamila, the guy was way out of her league.

Mid-afternoon, the bells on the door jingled. Liza entered carrying a giant platter of adorable mini cupcakes. The frosting looked like tiny hydrangea blossoms.

"Wow!" Patty came down from the stepladder. "Those are so cute."

Her sister placed them on the counter. "Thanks. I made them for Tessa this morning."

"You did? I didn't see you baking."

"I got up super early and went to Rebecca's house. She loves to bake, too."

"Nice." Patty reached for a cupcake. "Can I try one?"

"Sure. Take a pink. You'll like it the best."

Liza had gone back to being her sweet self, thank goodness.

She plucked a pink cupcake from the edge of the circle and ate it in one bite. "Oh my gosh. Delicious." Patty took a second one before even swallowing the first.

Tessa came out of the storeroom, and her face lit up. "Those are gorgeous, Liza."

"They're for you. To thank you for being so nice to me."

"Really? That's so lovely." She selected a blue one and took a small bite, licking frosting off her upper lip. "What do I taste? Something flowery?"

"It's rosewater." Liza glowed. Pleasing others was her superpower.

The bells jingled again, and a woman entered. She had on

navy blue cropped pants, a white blouse, and Gucci loafers. "Hello."

Tessa patted her lips with a napkin. "Welcome. Can I help you find anything special?"

"Do you carry Hawk and Winters wines? I tasted one the other night, and I'd like to take some home."

Patty expected her to suggest the woman drive out to the winery.

"I have a few in the back. Pinot Noir, I think."

She's going to sell her brother's stash?

"That's fine," the woman said. "I'll take a case if you have it."

"I'll see what I've got." She glided into the storeroom as calm as soft breeze.

While clever Tessa went in search of the wine she refused to carry, Patty kept the customer occupied. "Would you like to sample some cheese? Our premium Gouda is from the Netherlands."

The woman plucked a square off the tray with a toothpick. "Mmm, delicious. And oh my, those are the most darling cupcakes I've ever seen. May I?"

Liza balked, but she lifted the tray and smiled. "Oh, um, sure."

The customer gingerly selected one with lavender frosting and bit into it. She wrinkled her forehead. "Interesting. I detect a hint of orange zest and rosewater."

"Wow, exactly. There's a bit of both."

The woman fixed her eyes on the little cakes. "I'll take a dozen, doesn't matter what colors." She waved a hand over them.

"Oh, they're not for…"

Patty cut her off. "Certainly. Liza will box them for you. They're two-fifty each."

"That's all?" the customer said. "I was expecting twice that."

Tessa returned with a box. "I have six bottles. If you want more, let me know. We can ship."

"Wonderful." The woman put her credit card on the counter. "You can start ringing me up. I just need some snacks for the drive home."

"Where are you from?" Tessa asked, slipping each bottle into brown paper bags before placing them in a carrier.

"Monterey. It's not far, but we have the grandchildren with us." She tossed expensive gourmet treats onto the counter as if she were buying gas station candy.

Patty rang up the items. In all, the total came to almost four hundred dollars.

She handed the customer a white bag full of snacks and a clear plastic box with the cupcakes.

Tessa's eyes widened when she saw the container of cupcakes, but she followed the woman out the door without comment.

When the door closed, Liza glowered at Patty. "I can't believe you sold Tessa's cupcakes."

"At that price, yeah. Believe me, she'll be thrilled. If there's one thing I've learned from her, it's that everything's for sale at the right price."

The shop owner returned with a huge grin. "I wish we had more customers like *Miss Monterey* there. What did you charge for the cupcakes, Liza?"

"Patty priced them at two-fifty a piece, which is outrageous. They're so easy to make."

Tessa grabbed the calculator and started punching numbers, her lips tight and brow furrowed. "I want to sell your mini-cupcakes at the Fourth of July picnic. Can you decorate red, white, and blue?"

"Of course," Liza said. "But I'll be long gone by then."

"Can you stay? It'll be worth it. Your cupcakes will be a hit."

"I, uh, I…"

Patty shook her head. "Liza has to go home. It's almost July, and she needs to get organized to go back to school."

Her sister would no doubt love to stay, and Tessa's offer was generous. Patty couldn't deal with another change in plans.

"Gee, Patty," Liza said. "I could stay longer. Fall semester doesn't start until September."

"Then of course you'll stay." Tessa clapped her hands as if it were a done deal.

"I'm sorry, but neither one of us is staying much longer. Cece's getting her cast off, I'm going back to LA, and Liza needs to spend time in Texas before she goes back to school. We all need to return to our regular lives." She held out her hands like a crossing guard stopping traffic.

What was her regular life? It didn't matter; she had to plant her feet on sturdy ground. She'd suffered too many changes, stressors, and unexpected events. Every time Liza postponed her trip home, Patty had to recalibrate. Her free-spirited outlook on life was gone. She craved stability. "And besides," she said, focusing on practical matters. "We've both stayed at Cece's too long already. If not for her broken wrist, I'd have left weeks ago."

"I can solve that. The apartment's empty."

"What apartment?"

The shop owner pointed to the ceiling. "The one above our heads. It's sort of a loft. Bedroom, bathroom, utility kitchen. Perfectly fine place for a short-term stay."

Liza encircled her arms around her waist. "It sounds nice."

Patty clenched her teeth. "No. It's time for Liza to go back to Texas!"

Tessa drew back. "Well, it seems I've touched a nerve. I'm sorry I even brought it up."

Liza ran out the door.

Patty felt smaller than the tiny person she was. She'd hurt her sister's feelings and embarrassed herself in front of Tessa, who'd only ever been wonderful to her. "I'm sorry, Tessa." She hung her head like a guilty dog.

"Listen, I understand you've been through a lot. But you need to pull it together. You're acting crazy. My God, if I had a sister like Liza, I'd beg her to stick around as long as she could."

The admonition stung.

Liza had made it clear how she ached to be part of her life. Why did Patty keep pushing her away?

18

Even Cece chose a side, and it wasn't Patty's.

"What do you care if she stays a couple more weeks? Especially if she's not staying here?"

They sat in the family room, after dinner eating mocha chip ice cream from the carton.

Noah was asleep, Brad was working late, and Liza was nowhere to be seen.

She hadn't spoken to her since she'd run out of the shop in tears.

Shadow purred, snoozing against her leg.

Patty stroked the cat's soft fur. "I don't get it. Liza and Tessa hardly know each other. Isn't it weird that she'd invite her to camp out upstairs from the shop when they only just met a few weeks ago?"

"No," her friend said. "It's not weird. This is Clearwater. People do nice things for other people all the time."

Patty took the container of ice cream and ate more. "Whatever."

"Can't you see how much Liza adores you? All she wants is

your approval and attention. She's very grown up in some ways, but a child in others."

"Maybe." She shifted, disturbing Shadow. The cat crawled over her legs and settled against a pillow.

"Here's what I think," Cece said. "There's more to Liza's being here than a plan that fell apart. I hang out with girls her age every day. I can tell when there's more to the story than what they're willing to reveal."

"Maybe," Patty said, mulling over Cece's analysis of her sister's situation.

Her friend put the lid on the ice-cream container. "All I know is Liza needs something, and she needs it from you."

She sighed. Whatever her sister needed from her, she was in no way equipped to provide it.

Three days later, Liza moved to the loft apartment above Mariano's Cheese and Wine.

It was the beginning of summer, and a bustling atmosphere emerged around Clearwater.

Kids hung out on the playground, wine tours brought tourists into town, the Chess-in-the-Park Club kicked off their season, and an old-fashioned ice cream truck drove up and down the streets jingling, *Yankee-Doodle.*

Despite the beautiful weather, a dreary cloud settled over Patty, as she helped her sister move. With a bag in each hand, she followed Liza through Mariano's storeroom and up the stairs.

"It's really nice." Her sister's suitcase thumping on each step. "And I did some reorganizing yesterday."

The stairs ended at a small landing in front of a door.

Liza pushed it open. Sunlight flooded the entry.

Patty squinted, as she walked into the studio apartment. It was the size of an average bedroom, but bright and cheery, with a hardwood floor and clean white walls. Two windows looked over the park. The view was lovely.

She sat on the twin bed tucked into the corner, running a hand over the soft blue comforter. Next to the bed was a nightstand with a lamp and a box of tissues.

A bookshelf, a club chair, and a tiny round table with two chairs completed the furnishings. It was even nicer than her condemned duplex in LA.

"Is there a bathroom?"

Liza pointed to a closed pocket door. "Right over there."

Patty poked her head in. Even the tiny bathroom was cute. "It's great, Liza, very cozy. You did a good job setting it up."

"Thanks."

"What about the kitchen?" she asked. It was nothing more than a sink, microwave, and mini-refrigerator. "You can't bake cupcakes here."

"I'm baking them at Tessa's house."

"Oh, right. That makes sense." She opened the door.

"Patty, wait. You're not mad at me, are you? I mean, I know you wanted me to go home and all, but I just..."

"I'm not mad at you." She sighed. "I'm just, I don't know, a little envious."

"Of me?"

Her body sagged. "I'm twenty-nine, and my life is in pieces. You're only twenty-one, and your life is on track. So, yeah, I guess I am jealous. But I'm still really proud of you. Graduating from Princeton next year—pretty amazing."

Liza's face darkened.

Had she said something wrong? "What's the matter?"

Her sister brushed it off. "Nothing. It's just that..." She seemed to force a smile. "You know what? Nevermind. You'd better go. Tessa needs you downstairs, and I have to unpack."

Now was her chance. Liza had given her a small opening.

She wanted to reveal something. Patty could step up and be the big sister Cece had told her to be.

Or not.

"Yeah, I have to get downstairs. Let me know if you need anything."

She gave her sister a quick hug and dashed out the door but then hesitated halfway down the stairs. Maybe she should go back and push Liza to open up.

Patty did an about face. Why was she unable to make a simple decision?

Her cell phone buzzed in her back pocket. She pulled it out and read a text from Tessa asking her to come to the shop.

"Huh, that's odd."

With the decision made for her, Patty trudged down the stairs. She pushed the swinging door harder than necessary and went into the shop.

"Tessa, did you…" She halted.

Adam was standing by the counter.

Her mentor gave her a conspiratorial look. "Adam was just telling me he heard somebody from Monterey had purchased Hawk and Winters wine from us."

"Really?" Patty picked up a neatly folded tea-towel and refolded it. "That's interesting."

"Why's it interesting?" Adam asked.

"Well, it's not really." She giggled, her poise slipping away.

He crossed his tanned, muscled arms over his chest. "Do you know anything about it?"

She held her palms up. "I'm, um, I'm not exactly…"

"Adam." Tessa intervened. "You know I don't sell your wine. Now, there was a woman here a few days ago, and she might've been from Monterey. Perhaps she bought your wine somewhere else and got mixed up as to where she got it. People do that all the time."

Unnerved as she was, Patty couldn't help but admire the way Tessa evaded the issue.

Adam scratched his beard. A smirk played on his face. "I guess I'll have to take you at your word. But you do know that selling my wine without an agreement between us is not a good way to do business."

"Of course I do."

Patty fiddled with her necklace. His fiery demeanor made him even more attractive. She wanted to be near him, to hear his voice, to smell his scent. She was drawn to him like a peahen to a peacock fanning his feathers.

"One more thing," Adam said. "And then I'll go."

"What?" Tessa asked, her voice icy.

"Is it true Kamila's going to work here?"

Her face grew dark. "How is that any of your business?"

"I guess it's not. But I suggest you have a serious talk with Sophia."

Patty took it all in. Liza wasn't the only one hiding something; Clearwater was rife with secrets.

"You're out of line, Mr. Hawk." Tessa pointed at his nose. "You had your chance to join the Mariano family five years ago. I suggest you go back to making wine and minding your own business. Your opinion is not only unwelcome, it's irrelevant."

Adam's chest expanded, and his jaw tightened. "I accept that my opinion is unwelcome. But I assure you, it is not irrelevant."

He stalked out.

The door slammed, and the bells jingled.

Patty expected her to call him a nasty name or complain about his meddling, but all she did was stare at the floor where he'd been standing.

"Are you okay?"

Tessa's head snapped up. "Can you close up tonight? I have something I need to take care of." She disappeared without waiting for an answer.

Patty's stomach churned. A storm was brewing, and she was at risk of heading right into the thick of it.

19

Several days passed with no mention of Kamila or the confrontation between Tessa and Adam.

Liza was settled in the loft and was busy buying ingredients for the cupcakes, so Patty's life returned to a semblance of normal.

Early on Monday morning, she received a call from a number she didn't recognize. She ignored it and finished making Noah's breakfast. "How about some scrambled egg, big boy?"

The toddler bounced in his highchair.

She sat in front of him and blew on the egg. "We have to let it cool."

Noah pounded on his tray. "Eat, eat!"

"Okay, just a…" Her cell buzzed again, and the same number came up. She put a little piece of egg on Noah's tray. "Hello?"

"Patty Sullivan?" a male voice asked.

"Yes?"

"I'm the new property manager at, uh, hold on, I got the address here somewhere."

Her heart thumped. "Property manager?"

"That's right. I just took over the property at…" There was a long pause.

There were voices in the background, like a busy office full of people talking on phones.

"Hello?" Patty said. "Are you still there?"

"Yep, just scrolling through the information. Gimme a sec…"

She couldn't take the suspense. "Can you just tell me the status of my apartment? I'd like to know when I can move back home."

"I understand," the man said. "Oh, wait, here it is. Hmm, it looks like, just let me change screens."

She waited, her foot tapping, and watched Noah drop pieces of egg to the floor where Shadow sat meowing for scraps.

"Here we are." The property manager sounded pleased. "Now it makes sense. You lived in a duplex that was red-tagged on, let's see, back in May I think it said."

"Yeah, that's right." Patty got excited. "Is it done? Is the ceiling fixed?"

"No ma'am. The property was sold."

She didn't care who owned it, she just wanted to go home. "But are the repairs done? Can I move back in?"

"It's not being repaired. That's why I'm contacting you. The structure is going to be torn down."

"Torn down?" Her stomach dropped. "Why?"

"Because whoever owns it gets to decide what do with it."

Patty jumped up from her seat. "Are you saying I can't move back?"

"That's right. But the good news is you're getting your security deposit back as well as a refund on your May rent. Where should I send the check?"

She couldn't believe he'd said '*good news*'. There was nothing *good* about anything he'd just told her. She recited Cece's address.

"Okie-dokie. Check should arrive in ten to fourteen days. Any questions?"

She had a million questions, but none came to mind. "No."

"Then we're all set," he said. "You have a great day."

Patty put her phone down. She pictured a wrecking ball crashing into the little duplex. How could someone just decide to tear it down?

She'd never been attached to the apartment. In fact, it was a dump. Somehow, all that mattered was the fact that she'd lost her home.

Cece waltzed into the kitchen. "Good morning!" She gave her a hug and Noah a kiss. "Today's the day."

"What day?"

"How could you forget?" her friend teased. "Today I get my cast off."

"Oh, yeah, that's right." She tried to sound happy.

"What's wrong? You look upset."

Patty stood. "Um, actually, I have a little headache." The last thing she wanted to do was put a damper on Cece's good mood. "But I'm fine. You ready for me to braid your hair?"

Cece's cheery smile vanished. "Maybe you should lie down."

"It's okay." She pulled out a chair for her. "Sit down and let me do your hair."

Standing behind her, Patty lifted the heavy brown curls and separated them. They were unruly, but she tamed them, winding them together until they formed a perfect tail on the back of her friend's head. She secured the end of the braid with a red band. "Cece?"

"Yeah?"

"Um…"

Cece faced her. "What is it, Patty? What's wrong?"

She swallowed the words. This was a good day for her friend, and it would be selfish to spoil it. As much as she wanted reassurance, not to mention sympathy, this wasn't the time to ask for it. “Nothing. I was just thinking we should do something fun later to celebrate you getting your cast off. Do you want to?”

“Yes.” Cece’s bright smile returned. Let’s do that.”

The hustle and bustle at Mariano’s distracted Patty from her crisis.

While Tessa organized an impromptu wine-tasting for a local PR company, Patty managed the steady stream of shoppers. But the moment she paused between customers, her mind dashed back to the fact she had nowhere to live.

In the late afternoon, the shop quieted, and she called Cece.

The delight in her friend’s voice warmed her heart.

“So, the cast is off?”

“Yes! And it feels so good. I finally can scratch my arm!”

“Yeah, well, I hope you’re not planning to go back to yoga anytime soon.”

Cece laughed. “Very funny. Hey, I know we talked about doing something tonight, but Brad wants to go to dinner in the city. Do you mind?”

“Of course not. Do you need me to pick up Noah from Julia’s?”

“It’s okay. We’ll get him on our way home. You, my friend, can take the night off.”

With the night free, Patty stayed at Mariano’s to assist with the last-minute tasting. It was a good thing, too, because Tessa was not herself. At one point, she mixed up a Malbec and a Merlot, and Patty had to step in, deftly switching the bottles and whispering the correction in Tessa’s ear.

It was after ten when they finished cleaning up.

“Thanks for staying. And for catching my mistake. I’m not on my game tonight.”

“Everything okay?” Patty asked, fairly certain it wasn’t.

"Just too much going on."

Tessa hadn't said a word about Kamila since Adam's warning, so she didn't either. Besides, with her apartment about to be hit with a wrecking ball, there were far more important things to worry about.

"Can you let Liza know I ordered the cupcake pans?" Tessa dried the last wineglass and hung it on the rack. "She can start baking anytime. A thousand little cupcakes—it'll take her at least a week."

"I guess." She pictured her sister hanging out in Tessa's kitchen

"All right, then." The shop owner slipped her sweater on inside-out. She either didn't notice or didn't care. "Thanks again. See you tomorrow."

The door closed, and Patty let out a puff of air. She was tired and drained and hungry. With the stress over her soon-to-be demolished apartment, which she'd suddenly become very fond of, her stomach had been in knots all day.

Her stomach gurgled. She needed food, and she needed it fast.

With no drive-thru places in Clearwater, she had to travel fifteen minutes away to the closest McDonalds.

As she waited in line with her motor running, her phone buzzed. A number she didn't recognize lit up the screen.

"Seriously?" She ignored it. Her day had started with a call from a strange number and didn't want to end it the same way.

When whoever it was called right back, she decided to answer. If it was more bad news, what difference would it make?

"Hello?"

"Patty?" The voice was familiar, but she couldn't quite place it.

"Yes?"

"It's Adam Hawk."

She hit the break hard. The jolt threw her against her seatbelt. "Ouch."

"Are you okay?"

"Oh, um, yeah." She exited the drive-thru line and pulled over, adrenaline soaring. "How are you?"

"I'm fine, but you need to come over to my place. I have your sister here. There's been a little problem."

20

A long, winding driveway off of a dark road led to Adam Hawk's house. Her heart thundered.

"Holy Cow," she said to herself.

The sprawling ranch-style house had white wood siding and a wide porch with six rocking chairs, three on either side of the front door. All around the property were endless rows of grapevines illuminated by a full moon.

She parked behind a large black truck and looked in her rearview mirror. The long, stressful day had taken a toll. She applied a light swipe of lip gloss and finger combed her hair. Thankfully, she hadn't spilled red wine on her denim dress or clean white sneakers.

The door opened before she even knocked.

Adam's broad shoulders filled the doorway. "Hey."

"Hi." She followed him inside.

"Can I get you anything?" he asked.

"No thanks, I just, um, I'd better see Liza."

Adam led her through the entry way and into a warm kitchen. It had exposed beams, hardwood floors, and reclaimed wood cabinets. A round copper fixture hung over the center island. The room smelled like melted butter and toast.

The kitchen opened into a den where her sister and Rebecca were asleep on the sofa. Both had on very short dresses and remnants of too much make-up.

Tipsy lay between them, snuggled against the dog walker's leg. He wagged his tail and lifted his head.

"Thank you for bringing them here. Liza's not exactly a worldly girl."

"Rebecca probably isn't worldly either. It's pretty isolating, you know, living in a small town. Soon as kids get a taste of what's out there, they push the limits. I certainly did."

"Me, too." She sat beside Liza and smoothed her hair. She could smell the alcohol.

"They both got sick on the way back here. A few times. So, I don't think they'll throw-up anymore. But I've got trashcans handy, just in case."

"Where'd you say they were? In some bar?" She couldn't imagine her little sister going out drinking.

Adam sat on the edge of a brown leather recliner and leaned forward, his hands folded. "Yep, a Western bar about twenty minutes outside of town. I went to grab a beer with a buddy of mine. When we walked in, Liza and Rebecca were line-dancing, hanging out with a few guys. No big deal."

"Sounds like fun." She rubbed the back of her neck. Her shoulders were tense and sore.

"About an hour later, there was all this commotion, and it looked like they were in the middle of it. Turned out some guy hit on Liza and got a little touchy, so she shoved him."

"Unbelievable. That is *so* not Liza."

He chuckled. "Yeah, she doesn't look like a bar fight kind of girl. Anyway, before it got out of hand, my buddy and I made them leave. Rebecca cried all the way home, begging me not to drop them off at her mom's house. That's how we ended up here."

Patty absorbed the story. Her sister had been perfect for twenty-one years. She had to mess up eventually. Good thing somebody trustworthy was there to stop the fall.

The dog walker's pocket chimed.

Patty reached for the cellphone.

The text was from Rebecca's mother.

Where are you?

Patty typed in a short, and true, answer.

With Liza and Patty. Staying over. All good.

It hadn't been all that long since she'd needed to cover her own tracks with her parents. She still knew how to bend the truth without breaking it. Rebecca's mother responded with a thumbs up and heart emoji.

She sent back a kissy face.

Liza lifted her head. "Patty?" Her voice was raspy. She licked her lips.

"Hey. You okay?"

"Where are we?" Her little sister rubbed her eyes with both hands.

"We're at Adam's house. I'm gonna take you and Rebecca home." Patty glanced at Adam. He sat in a leather chair with his elbows on his knees paying close attention.

"I lub you, Patty." She yawned. "I lub you so mush."

"I love you, too, Liza-cake," she said, using her father's pet name. That was what he'd called them both.

His two little cupcakes—Patty-cakes and Liza-cakes.

She kissed her sister's cheek, then untangled herself and stood. "Can I use your bathroom?"

"Sure." Adam pointed. "There's one by the front door."

Patty got into the bathroom before the tears came. She didn't even know why she was crying, except she was hungry, tired, and emotionally drained.

And oh yeah, homeless.

She was entitled to a good cry.

Patty turned on the water and let it run while she used the toilet and gave in to a short but cathartic blubbering.

Then she washed her hands in cold water, taking in the minimal décor of the powder room. Same wood floor as the kitchen, a plain white sink with cabinet below, two dark gray towels on the towel bar, and a bar of soap on a chipped saucer.

As she dried her hands, she looked in the mirror. Traces of mascara had smudged below her eyes. She tried to clean it off with toilet paper and water.

It didn't work, so she added a tiny bit soap which got into her eyes and burned like fire. "That was so stupid," she told her reflection. She bathed her eyes in water until the sting subsided.

Patty returned to the kitchen, where Adam stood in front of the stove, a spatula in his hand.

"Are you hungry?" he asked, glancing over his shoulder.

Tipsy sat at his heel, tail thumping.

"Oh, um…" she pushed on the corner of her eye before it even started twitching. "I really should take the girls home. They've caused you enough trouble already, and it's so late, and I have to be…"

"Slow down." He turned off the gas burner. "They're sound asleep."

Patty looked at the sofa, Rebecca on one end and Liza on the other, both covered with beautiful crocheted blankets. "Are those handmade blankets?"

"Yep." He tipped the frying pan, and two toasty sandwiches slipped onto a heavy wooden board. "My mom was quite the crafter. I must have a dozen sweaters and twice as many knit scarves."

"Was?"

"She died a few years ago."

Her eyes filled up again. "My dad died four months ago."

Adam nodded. He sliced the sandwiches. "Yeah, Liza said something about that. I'm sorry."

She stepped closer.

The Greek god was almost a foot taller than her.

"Smells good," she said. "And I'm starved."

They sat on stools at the end of island.

Adam opened a bottle of red wine and poured two glasses.

Patty ate one of the small triangles, cheese oozing through the crusty edge. "Delicious. Cheddar and what? Gruyere?"

He smiled with approval. "You're good."

"I know my cheeses." She tasted the wine. "Perfect pairing, too."

"It is. Grilled cheese calls for something dry and acidic." He tilted his glass and studied the wine. It was dark purple, like ink. "This is an Argentinian Malbec."

They ate and drank and talked about wine until Adam circled back to his mother. He licked his lips. "I miss my mom. She was the glue that held everyone together. And now my dad's about to get remarried." He looked directly at Patty. "It's funny that he can replace his wife, but I can never replace my mom."

Tears dribbled down her cheeks. She'd never be able to replace her father either.

"Oh, geez." He pushed his fingers through his hair. "I didn't mean to make you cry."

Patty sniffled and wiped her eyes with a napkin. "You didn't. I cry all the time now, which is *so* not me. I really hate it."

Adam put a hand on her back. "I understand."

She lost herself in his gray-blue eyes. "I got some bad news today. My apartment's going to be bulldozed."

"The place where the bathtub fell through the ceiling?"

"You heard about that, huh?"

"Yeah, I did."

Patty took a piece of sandwich and ate it in two bites. "Anyway, I don't know what I'm going to do. I was planning to go home, but now I don't have a home to go to."

"You'll figure something out." It sounded cliché, but coming from him, it didn't. His voice held a note of certainty.

"Maybe." She rubbed her forehead. "I'm not very good with crises."

"You know, sometimes it takes a kick in the ass for people to realize they need to move in a new direction, choose a new road. Sounds like you just got that kick."

"Wow." She whispered the word. "That was insightful."

"Not really, it's just how life works." Adam tipped his glass back and swallowed the wine.

"You make it sound easy."

"It's not, believe me, I know that from experience."

Patty tried to read his expression, but it gave away nothing. "Sounds like you might have had your own kick in the ass."

He faced her, and his eyes darkened. "I've had several." He leaned in and put a hand on her cheek. His thumb brushed over her lips.

She stopped breathing. His lips touched hers so softly she barely felt it, but it rocked her down to her toes.

21

Patty jumped off the stool. "I need to go. Have to get those girls home."

Adam stood, a tiny smile on his lips. "Okay. I'll help you."

While she helped Rebecca, who was groggy but able to walk, Adam scooped Liza up and carried her like a baby.

Seeing how easily he'd lifted her sister made her dizzy. The kiss still tingled.

Patty played it cool and tried to hide the jitters brought on by his sexy, masculine presence.

Once both girls were situated and buckled in, she glanced at Adam. "I can't thank you enough."

"Maybe I should follow you in my truck. I think you're going to need help getting them inside."

"Really?" She hadn't even thought about that.

"Yeah. My mom taught me a man always makes sure a woman gets home safely. In this case, three women."

"That's so nice. Thank you."

"No problem." His off-kilter smile appeared. "So, Brad and Cece's house?"

"We'll go back to Mariano's. Liza's been staying in a little loft above the shop."

"Oh, okay," Adam said, a crease between his eyebrows. "I'll see you there."

It was a fifteen-minute drive back to town.

Patty kept glancing in her rear-view mirror to see if he was really behind her.

He was.

She parked behind the storeroom and looked in the back seat.

Both girls were sound asleep.

Adam pulled up next to her and got out of his black pick-up truck. He reached into her car and maneuvered Liza out first.

"Is she heavy?" she asked, concerned for his back.

"Heavier than she looks, but don't tell her I said that."

Patty led him up the stairs. She turned on a dim light as he gently set Liza on the bed.

The action reminded her of their father. He'd always kept his girls safe.

"One down," Adam said. "One to go."

"Right." She tried to hide the tremor in her voice.

The moment he left, Patty ran to the sink, filled two mugs with water, and popped them in the microwave. The least she could do was offer him tea. She arranged some cookies on a plate.

The microwave pinged, and when she removed the mugs of boiling water, some splashed on her hand. "Youch!" She ran her left hand under cold water and tore open tea bags with her right hand and teeth.

By the time Adam made it back upstairs, she had everything in place.

He put a snoring Rebecca next to Liza and straightened his back with a grunt. "Well, it's been a while since I carried a drunk girl up those stairs."

Patty blinked. "What d'you mean?"

He ran his hands through his thick hair. "Kamila. We used to, um, we were together for a while. You probably already knew that."

"Oh, right, yeah—do you want tea?"

"Sure." Adam sat at the small dinette table. With his long legs, he looked too big for the chair.

The dim overhead fixture cast a warm glow around the room.

Patty put the tea and cookies on the table and sat next to him.

He ate a shortbread cookie, then pointed to the angry red spot on the back of her hand. "What happened?"

She lowered her hand into her lap. "Nothing. Just a little burn."

"It wasn't there earlier." He picked up her hand to inspect it. "Does it hurt much?"

Patty gulped. She nodded.

"You need to keep it cool." He went to the sink and soaked a few paper towels in water. Adam sat in the chair across from her and placed the compress on her hand. "Keep that there for a few minutes. Helps with the sting."

"My mom used to tell us to put butter on burns." Patty was so absorbed in the color of his eyes she forgot about the burn. Cold water from the compress dripped through the fabric of her dress onto her legs, but she didn't care.

Adam had enchanted her.

"Butter's an old-wives-tale. Cool water is best."

"Feels better already." She tried to stop looking at him, but her eyes wouldn't cooperate.

Adam glanced at his watch. "Wow. It's after two in the morning."

Patty's leg bounced up and down. She ate a cookie. She needed to know more about Adam Hawk. "Can I ask you a question?"

He reclined and crossed his legs. "Sure. I'm practically an open book."

She laughed.

He was more like a diary with a padlock on it.

"Are you and Kamila getting back together?"

Adam scratched his beard, and his eyes shifted toward the bed where Rebecca and Liza slept.

"I'm sorry." She regretted asking. "Your, um, personal life is really none of my business."

"It's okay." He tilted his head side to one side, cracking his neck. "I'm the one who brought her up, which I shouldn't have. It's just that this loft brings back my teen years, you know?"

Patty imagined Kamila and Adam in the bed, no doubt the place where they'd had their firsts of many things. "Sorry."

"It's my fault, really. Guys shouldn't talk to girls they like about their ex-girlfriends. It's bad form."

Girls they like—

The corner of her eye, which had been behaving up until that moment, twitched wildly. She dropped the compress and rubbed her eye, as if it were itchy not twitchy.

"Do I make you nervous?"

"Oh, uh, no, well, maybe a little." Between her jumping eye and bouncing knees, it was undeniable.

Adam set his mug on the table.

Patty admired the tattoo on his wrist. Without meaning to, she touched it. His skin was warm and smooth. "Are these grapevines?"

"Yes." He pulled his arm away. "It's late. I should go."

He stood, and she looked up at him.

She pinched her lips with her fingers and tried to stand, but her legs wouldn't move.

Adam leaned over her, his face hovering above hers. "Would you mind if I kissed you again?"

His question sent a surge of adrenaline into her system. She stood and licked her lips.

His mouth was warm and minty. He put a hand on the back of her neck and pulled her closer.

Goosebumps rose on Patty's skin. Adam parted his lips and wrapped an arm around her waist.

In her almost thirty years and many, many kisses, she'd never been kissed like this—sensual, gentle, urgent.

A sigh escaped her throat. She leaned against his body, and he tightened his hold.

If not for the two girls in the bed, Patty would have dragged him over there.

Adam lifted his head and sighed. "Thanks for the tea and cookies." He stroked her cheek, his fingers trailing along her jaw bone. "Goodnight."

Then he was gone, vanishing like a spirit in the night.

22

Patty slept in the chair next to the bed. She woke up with a stiff neck and the delicious memory of Adam's kiss.

He had her head spinning.

She stretched and yawned, then peeked out the window.

At the park, a jogger ran along the path, and an old man sat on a bench with a steaming cup of something, reading the morning paper.

Rebecca groaned and raised her head. She looked around, confused, then bolted upright. "Oh my God, my mother's going to kill me. Where's my phone?"

"Right there." She pointed to the nightstand. "I texted your mom last night pretending to be you."

The dog walker reached over Liza and grabbed it. She squinted at the screen. "This is perfect, even the kissy-face emoji."

"I figured it would work," Patty said. "Lucky for you guys Adam was there last night."

Rebecca covered her face with both hands. "Oh, God, that's right. It was Adam. I'm so mortified!" She fell back against the pillows. “I have the worst headache, and my mouth feels like sandpaper.”

“Remember this next time you go out partying.”

“Don’t worry, I will.” The girl wiped her mouth with the back of her hand, her hair sticking out in all directions. “I feel like I’ve been dragged through dirt. What day is it?”

“Tuesday. Listen, I gotta run. Tell Liza I’ll see her later.” Patty pulled on her sneakers and left.

Outside, in the light of day, the events of the night before were like a dream.

Had Adam Hawk really been upstairs drinking tea with her, soothing the burn on her hand, kissing and caressing her?

She chastised herself for being such a sap. A couple of kisses probably meant nothing to him.

However, Adam’s kindness and chivalry stuck in her mind.

Patty drove straight to Cece’s, hoping she could slip in without being noticed.

No such luck.

In the kitchen, Brad and Cece sat at the table drinking coffee. They looked up, surprised.

Brad grinned. “Late night?”

“Don’t ask. My perfect little sister got herself into trouble.”

Cece’s eyes opened wide. “What happened?”

Patty helped herself to coffee. “She and Rebecca went out, drank way too much, and almost started a bar fight.”

Her friend’s mouth dropped open. “That doesn’t sound like Liza.”

Brad wore a fatherly frown. “How’d you find out? Did she call you?”

“Um—yeah.” Patty had no intention of mentioning Adam. “Anyway, I got them back to the loft, and then I just crashed in a chair.”

Noah’s little voice came through the monitor. “Ti-ti, Ti-ti.”

“There’s our little guy.”

"No you don't, missy." Cece raised her newly released right arm. "I'm back on duty."

"Look at you! I totally forgot. You finally have your arm back."

Cece moved her wrist around in circles. "Good as new," she said, giving Patty a hug. "Thank you for being my back-up all these weeks. Don't know what I would've done without you." She planted a sloppy kiss on her cheek and sprinted away.

Patty wiped her face.

Brad was eyeing her suspiciously. "What's wrong?"

She bristled and rubbed her left eye. "What makes you think anything's wrong?"

Brad crossed his legs. He put his coffee cup down with a clunk. "I can tell. I can always tell. I'm the father of a nineteen-year-old girl, and a man who's known a lot of women. Plus, I'm a lawyer. I read body language and facial expressions for a living. Ergo, I'm looking at *you*, and something is definitely wrong."

Patty coughed on the lump in her throat.

"Not to mention your eye's twitching like crazy. You've visited us a thousand times, and I've never seen that twitch before now."

She took her hand away from her face and let her eye go wild. "It's a nervous twitch from childhood. Went away when I left home, but it came back when I went to Dallas for my father's funeral."

He nodded. "That's understandable."

She sat at the table. "Then I broke up with the guy I'd been dating because I found out he was married."

Brad frowned. "Cece never mentioned that."

"I told her not to say anything. I was so embarrassed." Patty pulled her knees into her chest.

"Well." He rubbed the dark stubble on his chin. "That is rough."

"And after that, just when I was starting to feel better, my car got smashed by a hit-and-run driver." Reciting her list of woes was cathartic.

"I didn't know about that either."

"Have you seen my car?" Patty gestured toward the front yard. "It's been parked in your driveway for two months."

He raised a shoulder. "Yeah, but I just figured you'd backed into a wall or something."

She pouted. "Well, I didn't. Somebody hit my car and didn't even leave a note. Who does that?"

"Most people." Brad's smile was cynical.

"I guess." Patty withered like an old balloon. "And let's see, something happened right after that, what was it now? Oh yes," she put a finger in the air, "a bathtub fell through my ceiling and almost killed me." A flood of tears sprang forth. "So, so I came here. But then Cece broke her arm and Liza showed up and Tessa hired her cousin…" Patty tried to stop, but she couldn't. The words and sobs kept coming like cars on a freight train. "And yesterday I found out my apartment is going to be knocked down!" She hic-cupped then wiped snot from under her nose with her hand. "And—and last night Adam kissed me!"

Brad stood and took a step back. He looked like he'd stumbled upon a wild animal in the jungle. Evidently, his vast experience with women hadn't prepared him for a full-on *Patty Sullivan* break-down.

His stunned reaction made her cry even harder, mortified she'd spilled the beans.

"Adam kissed you?" he whispered.

She sniffled as she nodded.

"Why?"

"Why?" Now they both were whispering. "Because he likes me."

"Oh, right." Her friend's husband cleared his throat. "I'm

sure he does, but he's got a lot of baggage with that ex-girlfriend of his. You don't want to find yourself in the middle of that."

"I know. The last thing I need is to get caught up in that mess."

"What mess?" Cece came into the kitchen with Noah in her arms.

Patty turned.

"Oh my God, what's the matter? Why're you crying?" She handed her son to his father.

Patty covered her face. If only she'd stayed in town and gone straight to work, avoiding Cece until the crisis passed so she wouldn't be burdening her best friend, not to mention her best friend's husband, with any more of her problems. She blew her nose into a paper napkin. "It's nothing. I'm just being ridiculous."

Cece shook her head. "No, you're not." She shot a look in Brad's direction. "Did you make her cry?"

He held his hands up. "I, I don't really know."

"Brad didn't make me cry." She wiped away the last of her tears.

"Then what did?"

Patty hung her head. "Everything."

"I don't understand. What can I do?"

Noah squirmed, and Brad let him down.

He toddled over and wrapped his little arms around her leg.

She picked him up and embraced him. What was it she'd heard Brad say to Cece weeks ago—the night she eavesdropped on their conversation?

Patty will deal with her problems when she's ready.

It was time to be ready.

She lost focus. Her thoughts trailed, as if she were standing with one foot in the air, poised to take a step but unsure which way to go.

Every path she'd chosen in life had been a default decision, a way to escape from a place she didn't want to be.

Every single time, the road she chose led nowhere.

In a few months, she'd be thirty. She needed to find the road to the place she wanted to be.

Patty put the baby down and straightened her back. "You can't do anything, Cece. I'm the one who has to do it. And I'll start by packing up my stuff. I need to go home and deal with my life." She took a step, the first step in the direction of her road to somewhere.

23

Patty's road to somewhere was not a straight shot. It was Tessa who pushed her off track.

"Absolutely not," she said, coming down from the step-ladder. "You cannot leave Clearwater."

"Yes, I can. And I have to. I've been living in Cece's house for almost two months, which was fine when she had her arm in a cast. But that situation has ended. I'm no longer needed, and so, I must go." She raised her chin, feeling as if she had made an important pronouncement. "Besides, I do have a morsel of pride left in me." Her little speech was eloquent and convincing. Wasn't it?

Tessa would have none of it. She narrowed her eyes like a chess player calculating her next move. "Well listen up, Mary Poppins, Cece might not need you, but *I* do. Your decision to just up and go is putting me in a difficult situation."

Her budding confidence faded. "What d'you mean?"

"You owe me." She folded the step ladder with bang.

"I owe you?" Patty was intimidated by the charge.

"Sorry, that came out wrong."

"I'll say." She exhaled. "I don't understand where this is

coming from, Tessa. You knew I'd be leaving when you hired me." She almost mentioned Kamila, but that was a treacherous subject, and the last thing she wanted to think about was Adam's ex-girlfriend.

"You're right, but my expectations were low. As it turns out, you're a far better worker than I thought you'd be."

Patty crossed her arms. "That was a backhanded compliment if I've ever heard one. And I've heard a few."

"It's the truth. You're good. You work hard, you're reliable, and you have quite a knack for sales." Tessa uncovered a cheese tray left over from the wine-tasting. She nibbled a piece. "Plus, you have a natural talent. Your taste buds are highly sensitive, discerning. I see it in the way you pair foods, the look on your face when taste something new. It's a rare gift, and it should be nurtured."

She appreciated the compliment. She had no idea if Tessa was telling the truth or making it all up. Either way, it sounded good.

"And so, I'd like you stay another month."

"What? You're kidding, aren't you?"

"I'm not. You'll be doing me a huge favor. My assistant gets back at the end of July, so there's a definite end date."

Patty squeezed her eyes shut. Making minor decisions had become difficult; making major ones were near impossible. "I—I don't know what to tell you."

"Tell me you're staying." Tessa flung her arms open, as if it were the simplest thing in the world. "What're you rushing back to LA for anyway? A dead-end job at Pottery Barn? An apartment you can't even live in? Some guy?"

Just like that, the eye twitch returned. She pressed on it. "I like working at Pottery Barn," she said. "At least I did. I'm pretty sure I've been replaced."

Her friend raised an eyebrow. "Probably."

"And the last guy I dated was a total loser." Tears threatened, but Patty held them at bay. “And, if you must know, my apartment’s going to be knocked down, so essentially, I’m homeless.”

Surprise registered on Tessa’s face.

She expected a little sympathy, but instead she received another kick in the butt.

“See?” Tessa said. “You got nothing in LA. No job, no home, no guy. Do you even have any friends?”

She gawked. “That was mean.”

Tessa’s face softened. “I’m kidding. I’m sure you have friends.”

“Yeah, I do.” Patty’s voice squeaked. “A lot.”

“None like Cece though.” She’d got that one right.

There was nobody in the world like Cece.

She rubbed the corner of her eye. Tessa’s suggestion bounced around in her mind like a pinball. Stay in Clearwater another month?

Tempting, yet ludicrous.

“I don’t even know why we’re having this conversation. Sure, my life in LA sucks, but I gotta tell you, this place is stressing me out. I thought life in a small town was supposed to be quiet and simple, but it’s not. You can’t even sneeze without people knowing about it.”

Tessa took a green juice out of the mini-fridge. She divided it into two wine glasses and handed one over. “Drink. It’s good for you.”

Patty was not a fan of juice made primarily of spinach, but she followed the order.

“Come sit.” Tessa took her wrist and guided her to a table in the wine tasting area. She opened a package of cheddar-dill butter crackers, one of Patty’s favorite treats. “Listen, I’m not one to mince words.”

“I’m well aware of that,” she said, nibbling a cracker.

“I’m in a bit of a pickle.” The shop owner circled the rim of her glass.

"Okay." Patty tasted her green juice. It reminded her of freshly mowed grass.

"It's about Kamila."

She drank more green juice. "But I thought it was all arranged."

Tessa scratched her upper lip. "It is, or was, but I'm not sure it'll work out."

"Does this have anything to do with what Adam said the other day?"

"It could."

Patty rubbed her forehead with both hands. The situation became more interesting by the minute. And confusing. "So, have you hired her or not?"

"Well, I have, technically, but like I said, it might not work out. That's why I need you to stick around. Please."

"To do what? Babysit Kamila?" She was losing patience. "Geez, Tessa, for somebody who doesn't mince words, you're making minced meat out of this conversation."

"I know, and I'm sorry." She tapped a red fingernail on the table.

Tessa not in control of a situation was disturbing, and it made Patty anxious.

"The bottom line is, I don't think I can depend on my cousin. But I have to follow through—let the situation play out. My aunt's pressuring me big time. The whole thing's probably going to blow up in my face."

This sounded exactly like the kind of predicament Patty wanted to avoid. She drank more green juice, hoping it would give her the fortitude needed to tell Tessa *no*.

To tell her she was going home.

To tell her she had more than enough of her own problems.

"So…" Tessa's beautiful brown eyes widened with anticipation. "What do you say?"

Patty opened her mouth to say "*No*," but nothing came out.

She'd been poised to move forward, to take the first step, to deal with her life, but instead she took a giant step backwards into total indecisiveness. She dropped her head into hands. "I came here with a plan, and now I'm all messed up."

"I'm sorry. I realize I'm pushing you, but let me, your older and wiser friend, help you."

"Okay." She raised her head, hoping for some encouragement, maybe a teeny bit of support and understanding.

"You, my dear, are an unstable mess."

Patty shrank and readied herself for a hefty serving of tough love.

"You live in reaction-mode, responding to crises like a child playing hide and seek. You run and hide in a safe spot, until it's not safe anymore, then you take off in search of another safe place."

Her eye twitch revved up.

She recalled the number of times she'd moved in three years, how many jobs she'd had.

"And pardon me for pointing this out, but for an unstable person, you have a lot leaning on you. Cece needs you. Liza needs you. And now *I* need you."

Patty trembled.

Everything Tessa said was true.

"I have a proposal, so please, just hear me out." Her mentor put both hands flat on the table. "You keep working, and I'll give you a twenty percent raise. That'll give me time to sort through the Kamila situation."

Patty chewed her lip. She had no idea what that situation was, but maybe it didn't matter.

The offer was good, and it wasn't like she had a firm plan in LA. All she had were loose plans. In fact, she had no plans.

"Well, I do like working here." She fingered the silver moon charm on her necklace. "And I don't want you to have a problem with your cousin. But where am I going to stay?"

"What do you mean? You'll stay at Cece's."

"Oh, no." She shook her head. She needed to follow through on at least something. "I said I'd leave, and if I don't, I'd feel more pathetic than ever. That was my one big step forward today, deciding to leave Cece's house. I won't undo it."

"Then I'll throw in the loft upstairs as part of your compensation."

"But Liza's there."

"Only another week or so. And I'm sure she won't mind."

Patty stood and paced.

The loft was a cute and cozy for *one* person.

She and her sister would be on top of each other, just like they were when they were little sharing bunk beds.

Then again, Liza was scheduled to fly home on July sixth.

If she moved into the loft tomorrow, it would be exactly eight days.

Patty circled the table, picturing the two of them in one twin bed.

"I have a blow-up mattress at home that you can use until Liza leaves." Tessa had read her mind.

"Okay, fine." She gave in. "I'll do it."

"Good. Thank you, Patty. And just think, in one week, you'll have the place all to yourself. It's a perfect plan."

Perfect? Not quite.

24

Cece supported the new plan wholeheartedly. I think it's great." She dropped a load of clean, warm clothes onto Patty's bed. "And you can do your laundry here anytime."

It was a nice offer. But like a kid moving out of her parents' house, she needed to cut the cord. "Thanks, but I'm not bringing my laundry here. Besides, there's a washer and dryer in Tessa's storeroom."

"Even better." Her friend rolled up a pair of socks and tossed them to her. "I'm going to jump in the shower before Noah wakes up."

"I'll be here," Patty said. "And thanks for loaning me your suitcase."

"You're welcome." She kissed her cheek. "And just because you're camping out in Tessa's loft doesn't mean you can't come back here for a sleepover."

"I think I've exceeded my quota of nights in your guest room for the rest of the year."

"That, little missy, is not possible," Cece said. "Just so you know, you staying in Clearwater was the one and only upside to my broken wrist."

Patty looked into her friend's sapphire eyes, full of warmth and calm. "I'm glad I did. You do so much for me, you always have. Finally, I could pay back a little of it."

Cece tucked her hair behind her hears. She grew serious. "I know what people say, Patty. They say you're lucky to be my best friend."

"Of course they do." She chuckled. "I'm the one who tells them so."

"But you're wrong."

"What are you talking about?"

"I'm the lucky one." A wistful smile formed the edges of her lips. "When I met you, everything changed. You brought sparkle and fun into my life. Before you, I did nothing but eat, sleep, and study."

"I don't know about the sparkle." Patty tried to sound light-hearted. "But I did drag you out of the library a few times."

"More than a few." Cece blinked. Her eyes misted over. "I just want to tell you one more thing. Her friend's voice was firm. "There's no keeping score between us, but if there were, your side of the scale would weigh at least as much as mine. Probably more." She wiped a tear off her cheek and left the room, leaving Patty in stunned silence.

Liza welcomed her into the loft with an abundance of joy. She insisted Patty take the bed and she'd sleep on the blow-up mattress.

Together they rearranged the furniture, dragged a small book-shelf up from the store room, and made a cozy sitting area out of a couple of old beanbag chairs Tessa had brought from home.

It was shaping up. And with the loft being part of her compensation, she didn't feel like a freeloader.

A few days after Patty's official promotion, Kamila stopped by the shop. The two exchanged hasty hellos before Tessa, with forced cheerfulness, said she and her cousin were going to have lunch with Sophia.

"Come on." She put her hand on Kamila's back and ushered her to the door. "We don't want to be late."

Patty narrowed her eyes as they left. Everything about Tessa's behavior around her cousin and her aunt was disturbing. Her schedule had become erratic. And when she was at the shop, she was distracted and absentminded.

Concern over how she and Kamila would get along once they started working together discomfited Patty. She sensed a rivalry and suspected the dark-haired beauty had every intention of rekindling her relationship with Adam.

First loves were impossible to forget, especially one like Adam Hawk.

As it was, she'd done her best to forget about him, but the feel of his kiss lingered on her lips.

When she closed her eyes at night, she allowed herself to relive it—the taste of his mouth, the musky smell of his cologne, and the feel of his arms around her.

Every day when she walked in the park, stopped by Nutmeg's, or stepped outside onto the sidewalk, she was on the lookout for him.

Either her timing was off, or Adam had vanished.

On Friday afternoon, Patty walked out of Nutmeg's with her mid-day latte. She crossed the street and went into the park where Rebecca was walking her usual pack of dogs.

The girl waved with enthusiasm. "Patty, hi!"

"Hi, yourself. Have you recovered from your night out with my sister?" She knelt and scratched Tipsy under his chin.

Rebecca made a face and put a hand on her stomach. "It took a few days. Oh, man, was I sick. My mom thought I had the flu.

Thanks again for taking care of me. I kinda feel responsible for getting Liza into trouble."

"Liza's a big girl. And quite capable of getting herself into trouble."

"Did you ground her?"

Patty laughed. "I'm her sister, not her mother. Besides, I think the headache she had was punishment enough."

"I'll say." Rebecca rolled her eyes. She unhooked the dogs' leashes and let them romp in the grass. "I was so embarrassed when I saw Adam, but he was really nice about it."

It was the opening Patty'd been hoping for. "What'd he say?"

"Just that he was glad he and his friend were there to help us out. You know, he doesn't talk all that much, at least not to me, but he's not as much of a sourpuss as I thought. Maybe it's because Kamila is here." The dog walker raised her shoulders up to her ears and dropped them. "Of course, I'm the last person to understand relationships. I've never even had a real boyfriend."

Patty sipped her latte. "Do you know if Adam's around? I might've left my jacket at his house the other night. I thought maybe he'd drop it off at the shop, but—but I haven't seen him."

"He's out of town for a few days. Some wine thing at UC Davis. That's why Tipsy's staying with me. Hey, I have to go to his house and pick up more dog food later, you want me to look for it?"

"No, it's okay." Patty waved her off. "I'm not even sure it's there. Might be buried in my car under a pile of junk."

Tipsy barked. He stood on his hind legs and put his front paws on her knees.

Patty scooped him up. "How long are you dog-sitting?" she asked, faking indifference.

"Adam gets back tomorrow, I think. Or the next day, or maybe—you know what? I don't know. But for sure before the fourth of July. He's got that big party at the lake. Are you going?"

"I don't know anything about it." Tipsy licked Patty's chin as if it were coated in peanut butter. "What kind of party is it?"

"Fourth of July party. He does it every year." Rebecca put her fingers in her mouth and whistled so loudly everyone within earshot jumped. "It's a pretty big deal. He rents a tent and everything."

The dogs raced back and sat in front of her feet. She clipped their collars onto the leash.

Patty set Tipsy down. There was no reason Adam would invite her to his party. They hardly knew each other. "Well, I gotta run, Rebecca."

"Me, too. See you soon, and thanks again."

When she returned to the shop, Tessa was getting ready to leave.

"I have an appointment," she said. "And I'm not sure what time I'll be back."

"No problem." Patty had become accustomed to her mysterious outings and sudden departures. "I'll be here. Anything you want me to take care of?"

"I don't think so. Um, no, wait. The spicy mixed nuts—we're almost out. And maybe the black-truffle cashews." She waved a hand. "Just, just order whatever we need."

"I'll do it this afternoon."

"Okay, thanks." Tessa's face was pale. "You have no idea how much I appreciate your being here, Patty." She went out the front but came back ten seconds later and went out the back.

Patty downed the rest of her coffee, concerned. Tessa didn't know if she was coming or going.

She logged into their account with the nut company and ordered the spicy mixed, the cashews, and several other varieties. Without even checking, she knew exactly what was on the shelves and how much they had in inventory.

The bells jingled, and a UPS driver stuck his head into the shop. "Excuse me, I need you to open up the storeroom."

Patty closed the laptop. "I'm not expecting a delivery. What have you got?"

The driver looked at his paperwork. "Three cases of wine from a distribution center in Reno."

"That's weird. We usually take delivery direct from the winery."

"I'm just the driver. And I need to get moving, so could you please open the door?"

"Okay. I'll meet you around back."

She walked into the storeroom, unlocked the heavy sliding door, and pushed it open.

The driver handed her the paperwork and went to get his dolly.

She checked the *ordered by* line. It said, *Tessa Mariano.*

"Where do you want 'em?" he asked.

"Um, just right over there." She pointed to an area beside the walk-in cooler.

He stacked the plain brown boxes on the floor and held out a clipboard. "Sign here."

She did, hoping she wasn't making a mistake.

"Thanks," he said. "Have a nice day."

"You, too." Patty closed the door. She opened the box on top and removed one bottle. "What the…"

It was a bottle of Hawk and Winters Syrah.

The wine label had a gray-blue background—the color of Adam's eyes—and a hawk mid-flight with the sun behind it.

She opened the other two boxes, all Hawk and Winters Syrah—thirty-six bottles of it.

25

The cases of Adam's Syrah disappeared the day after they were delivered. Tessa never mentioned them, so Patty didn't either.

Maybe they weren't for the shop at all. Maybe Tessa had replenished her brother's supply now that he could store his own wines again. That was as good an explanation as any.

Still, it was another mystery gnawing at her.

In the days leading up to Fourth of July and the picnic on the lake, Patty worked harder than ever. The clearance sale at Pottery Barn was a walk in the park compared to Mariano's middle of summer sale and promotions. Tourists and visitors flocked to the gourmet store to taste, try, and buy.

She hardly had time to breathe and hadn't even seen Cece the day she moved into the loft.

Still, no sign of Adam.

The night of July third, Patty and Liza were in the storeroom decorating the last of the cupcakes. They'd set up an assembly line on a six-foot folding table.

Her sister piped red, white, and blue buttercream frosting onto the tiny cakes, then she stuck little American flag toothpicks into each one.

"I think these are going to be a hit." Tessa placed a tall stack of plastic containers on the table. She swiped a bit of frosting from one of Liza's pastry bags with her pinky finger. "Oh, yum. You really outdid yourself, Liza."

"Thank you." She squeezed her pastry bag and creating perfect little rosettes. "I did some calculations, and with everything we spent on ingredients, including wrappers and decorations and containers, the cost per cupcake came to less than fifty cents each."

"Seriously?" Patty found it hard to believe cupcakes could be so profitable. "I hope they sell as well as predicted."

"I do, too." Tessa closed a container with a click. "Carry on, girls. I'll be right back."

"Let's see if these taste as good as they look." Patty popped one into her mouth and savored the moist, light, lemon-y cake. She smiled. "You missed your calling, little sis."

Liza brushed hair off her face with the back of her hand. "I probably did." Her tone had an edge.

"What? Did I say something wrong?"

She shook her head. "No."

Patty knew every intonation of her sister's voice. "Liza, if there's…"

The sound of shattering glass startled them.

"Oh-oh. I'll be right back." She ran into the shop and found Tessa standing beside a pile of broken glass, green olives rolling around on the floor

"What happened?"

"I—I was going to make us a little snack. I opened the jar of olives, and it just slipped right out of my hand."

Liza came out of the storeroom. "Everything okay?"

"I made a mess, that's all."

"You don't look so good," Patty said.

Tessa held the edge of the counter. "I'm a little dizzy. I think I'm getting a migraine, which is weird because I usually only get them in the winter."

"You need to go home," Patty said. "I'll drive you."

"No, I can drive myself. Just let me…" She shut her eyes and put a hand on the left side of her head. "Okay, you can drive me."

"Good. Liza, you can finish up on your own, right?"

"Yeah, of course. And I'll clean the spill."

"I'm so sorry," Tessa said. "I can't believe I did that."

"It's nothing." Liza pulled a bunch of paper towels off the roll. "You guys go."

Patty grabbed her keys. She put a gentle hand on Tessa's back and guided her to the car.

Eight minutes later, they pulled into the driveway of Tessa's house. It had white siding, a raised porch across the front, and a sky-blue door. Trees surrounded it on all sides, and an old tire swing hung from a thick branch.

"Your house is lovely," Patty said, helping her out of the car.

Tessa mumbled something unintelligible. She held onto Patty's arm as they walked up the steps and into the house.

Buttercup greeted them at the door wagging her bushy tail.

"Hello, girl," Tessa patted the top of the dog's huge head and led Patty through the living room into the kitchen. She turned on the lights then hit the dimmer switch.

Catalogues, books, file folders, and plastic containers filled with assorted pastas covered the center island.

"Sorry about the mess." Tessa opened a bottle of pills sitting on the counter. She shook two into her hand and swallowed them with a sip of water. "Thanks for driving me."

"Of course. Anything you need me to do before I go?"

"No, I'm okay." She sat at the breakfast table with Buttercup's head in her lap. "Go home, go to bed. You have a big day tomorrow."

Tomorrow, the Fourth of July.

"Oh, right, the cupcakes. I guess you won't be there."

"I definitely won't. My headaches usually last a couple of days. Sorry to leave it to you."

"It's okay. Liza and I will handle it. You just feel better, okay?"

"I'll try." Tessa gave her weak, pained smile.

Patty was disturbed by the change in her friend. Tessa was in control of everything, but something had knocked her off kilter.

She was about to go when the cupcake pans placed in the drying rack caught her eye. She surveyed the modern kitchen with stainless steel appliances, double dishwashers, and fancy built-in ovens. "So, this is where Liza's been baking all week." Patty imagined her sister zipping around Tessa's kitchen as if she belonged there.

"Don't begrudge Liza."

The remark stung. "I didn't mean it that way. It's just kind of funny that this is the first time I've been in your house. I mean, I've known you for years."

"Yes, you have. But this is the first time you've been here when you're not stuck like glue to Cece."

Although the statement was true, Patty sensed criticism.

"It's good you're becoming more independent." Tessa squinted at her. "Better late than never."

"Thank you—I think."

Tessa stood and shuffled toward the stairs. She stopped and put a hand on the banister. "Good luck tomorrow. Don't give away too many samples."

"We won't." Patty smiled. As sick as she was, the shop owner still maintained a sense of control.

Tessa reached for her hand and squeezed it. "You're a wonderful friend, Patty. I hope you know that."

It was the nicest thing Tessa had ever said to her.

~

Patty struggled to go to sleep, listening to Liza's rhythmic breathing. When she finally did fall asleep, her dreams were a jumbled, confusing, hodgepodge of every bad thing that'd happened in the last five months.

The dream that shook her awake, however, involved Adam.

He was dressed in a tuxedo at a fancy party surrounded by beautiful women. Patty, wearing pajamas of all things, walked in.

Their eyes met.

Her feet floated above the floor as they glided toward each other. Closer and closer he came, his arms open.

Patty reached for him, but then just as he was upon her, the ceiling opened and a bathtub fell on top of her.

"Oh!" She bolted upright, her heart pounding.

What a bizarre and terrible dream. She flipped over her pillow and rested her cheek on the cool fabric.

Liza slept two feet away on the blow-up mattress. Her hair covered half her face, making her look like the girl she'd shared a room with for so many years.

She turned onto her back, stared at the ceiling, and tossed and turned for the next few hours.

At sunrise, Patty got up and put on jeans and a sweatshirt. She made herself coffee and took it with her to the park.

Outside, a cool breeze carried the scent of blooming flowers and fresh dew. She sat on a bench and watched the rising sun turn the sky into a swirl of orange and pink. She sipped her coffee.

A woman in black running pants and hooded jacket jogged in

her direction. The woman slowed as she approached. She stopped and put her hands on her knees, breathing hard.

"Are you okay?" The last thing she could handle was a medical emergency.

The woman held up a finger. Finally, she spoke. "God, I hate jogging." She sat on the bench and pushed off her hood. A long, dark ponytail spilled out. "Fancy meeting you here." Tessa's cousin smiled.

"Hello."

They traded glances. Patty sipped her coffee. It'd turned bitter.

"So, I hear you're gonna be my boss for a while."

"Is that what Tessa said?" She wasn't aware she'd have any actual authority over her.

"Pretty much. Originally, she said you were heading back to LA. But I guess your plans changed." It was a statement—not a question.

"They did." She fidgeted with her necklace as her teenage insecurities came roaring back.

Kamila stretched her neck. She crossed her ankles and looked straight ahead. "I can't believe I'm in Clearwater. I really thought I'd escaped for good."

An opportunity to learn more about Kamila *from* Kamila was too enticing to resist. She tested the waters. "I know what you mean."

"Do you?" The woman's eyes shifted.

"Kind of." She sipped her coffee and paused for effect. "I ran away from my hometown. The thought of going back there gives me hives."

Adam's ex-fiance nodded. "I don't exactly have hives, but coming back here was not part of my plan."

"Why did you then? If you don't mind my asking."

Kamila brushed a piece of lint off her leg. "I think I'd call it unfinished business."

Unfinished business, a euphemism for so many things, including and especially ex-boyfriends. If she was there to win back Adam, Patty wouldn't blame her.

"When do you start work?"

"In a couple days."

"Great. We need an extra set of hands. It's a busy place."

They both stood.

Kamila's height was as intimidating as her beauty. "I'm sure we'll work well together," she said.

"I'm sure we will." She tossed the remnants of her coffee into the grass. "Well, I need to take off. Big picnic on the lake today."

"Oh yes, the annual Fourth of July picnic. Maybe I'll see you there."

"Maybe." Patty extended her hand. "It was nice chatting with you."

"And you." Kamila grasped her hand with a firm grip.

Patty squeezed back.

26

By mid-afternoon, the lakeside lawn was covered in blankets and teeming with families, dogs, and picnic baskets.

Frisbees flew, and kites dotted the blue sky. The sound of wooden mallets striking croquet balls echoed.

To Patty's great relief, the cupcakes were a hit.

With Tessa stuck at home, she was in charge of sales while Liza passed out samples and sent everyone over to buy. The line grew so long even Cece stepped in to help.

"How are sales going?" Liza asked, refilling her sample tray with tiny bites.

"Unbelievable," Patty said. "Remember, only one taste per person."

Cece laughed. "Your sister's stingy with tastes."

"Just following orders."

Liza picked up the tray. "Don't worry. Okay, I'm going back in. Everyone who tastes wants more, so get ready for the next rush."

As her sister disappeared into the crowd, Patty scanned the park, squinting against the sun.

Still no sign of Adam. As much as she didn't want to, she couldn't stop thinking about him, especially since her conversation with Kamila.

She wiped her hands on her jeans. "Hey, do you know anything Adam's party tonight?"

Cece ate a vanilla cupcake and licked frosting from her lips. "I think it's a fundraiser for something." Her eyes widened. "Are you going?"

Patty shook her head. "I don't have money for that kind of thing. Besides, I haven't seen him in like a week." Her lips tingled at the memory of his kiss.

Cece nudged her. "Since he kissed you?"

"You know about that?"

"Of course I know. You think Brad can hide anything from me?"

"I can't believe he told you. Well, actually, I can." She sidled up to her friend. "You're really the only one I can trust with my secrets."

"Back at ya, missy." Cece snapped the lid on a container of cupcakes. "Looks like things are under control here, so I'm going to get Noah home for a nap. Don't forget, picnic dinner and fireworks by the lake tonight."

"I'll be there. And thanks again for helping out."

"My pleasure." Cece snatched a lemon cupcake and jogged away.

An hour later, the line dwindled to nothing. Everyone was down by the lake watching the mini-sailboat race.

Patty yawned. She put the cupcakes into the cooler and stretched out on the grass with a bunched-up sweatshirt under her head.

Warm sunlight bathed her face. The distant sounds of laughter and chirping birds blended into a soft, tranquil song.

She drifted away, inhaling the sweet aroma of Liza's cupcakes.

Patty had no idea how long she'd been asleep when the sound of panting woke her. She opened her eyes to Tipsy's nose. Was she dreaming?

Adam was standing over her.

She bolted upright. "Oh!"

He laughed. "Sorry. We didn't mean to scare you."

She shot to her feet. Smoothed her messy hair. "I can't believe I fell asleep. I was just so tired."

"Nothing like a nap in the sun."

Being near him made every nerve in her body flicker to life. Patty composed herself. "Very true."

"So, uh, Rebecca mentioned you left your jacket at my house the other night. I looked around, but I couldn't find it."

"Oh yeah. It was in my car, under the seat, behind a bunch of…" she was a terrible liar.

"Are you okay?"

Definitely not.

She inhaled and willed her pounding heart to slow down. It'd been a week since he'd rescued her sister, since the night of the kiss to end all kisses, since the night he didn't answer her question about Kamila.

Now he'd come to see her.

Tipsy stood on his hind legs, his front paws on Patty's knees. She picked him up and kissed the top of his head. Regardless of what she may or may not feel for Adam, she definitely had fallen for his dog. "I'm just embarrassed you caught me sleeping."

Adam rubbed his chin. "You looked so peaceful."

Her dry lips parted.

Peaceful?

There was nothing peaceful about her.

"Want to buy some cupcakes?" she asked.

He probably didn't. He'd obviously come to see her, to talk about the other night.

She looked up at him expectantly, gazing into his eyes and waiting for him to say whatever it was he came over to say.

"I do."

"You do what?"

"Want to buy some cupcakes."

"You do?" Patty hid her disappointment. "Great. How many?"

"How many do you have left?"

"About a hundred, mostly chocolate, I think." She opened a plastic container. "Here. Try one."

Adam popped the whole thing in his mouth.

Even the way he chewed was sexy.

He tasted the cake as if he were tasting wine, licking a dab of frosting off his lower lip. "They're delicious. I'll take whatever you have."

"You want a hundred cupcakes?"

Adam handed her two hundred and fifty dollars. "Yep."

"A hundred? Are you serious?"

"I am. I need them for the party tonight."

Ah yes, the party she wasn't going to. "Right. Cupcakes are a perfect party dessert."

"My late-harvest Syrah will pair beautifully with the chocolate."

She stacked the plastic containers on the table. "You want to count them?"

"You are an LA girl, aren't you?" Adam grinned. "I'm sure it's close enough. And I trust you."

She amused him. Or was he making fun of her?

Patty tucked a strand of hair behind her ear.

"Would you like to come?" Adam asked.

"Come where?"

"To my party. It starts as soon as fireworks are over."

She swallowed. "Maybe. How much are…"

"I'm inviting you to be my guest."

Patty opened her mouth, but no words came out.

"What do you say?"

Going to his party had *bad idea* written all over it.

"Um, well…" Her voice squeaked. She cleared her throat. "Okay."

"I'll see you later then." Adam smiled his crooked grin and winked at her.

27

"Relax, it'll be fine." Cece took a bite of potato salad. "And if it's not, you'll leave."

"I guess," Patty said, watching the sun slip into the lake. She picked up a pickle but before she could take a bite, her friend grabbed it from her.

"Don't eat pickles—too much garlic."

She set her plate down. "See that? I can't even think straight."

They sat in lawn chairs on the grass.

Noah climbed on Phil, as if his grandpa were a jungle gym, while Brad chatted with a friend.

"Patty," Julia said, taking a seat, "is Liza joining us?"

"I have no idea." She looked around. She hadn't seen Liza in hours. "She's probably hanging with Rebecca."

The sky turned black. Stars dotted the night sky, and the fireworks show began with a deafening boom.

Patty hugged her knees. "I can't believe I've never been here for the Fourth of July."

"You've been invited every year." Cece elbowed her. "Now we'll make it a tradition."

"Right," she said, trying to enjoy the show. All she could think about was Adam's party. She wished she'd declined his invitation.

"Stop bouncing your leg," her friend said. "It feels like we're having an earthquake."

"I'm just nervous about tonight. I should go change, right?"

Cece gave her a once-over. "Yes. You have crumbs stuck to your shirt and frosting in your hair." She grabbed her hands. "And when was last time you had a manicure? You'd better scrub those nails, missy."

Patty stood. "Well, thank you for being honest. I'm gonna go." She dropped the blanket over her friend's head.

"Have fun. Be good!" Cece said from under the blanket.

Back in the loft, Patty took a hot shower, pulling on strands of hair to remove bits of dried frosting.

She tried on a dozen outfits.

Nothing worked, and by the time she settled on a short red dress that needed ironing, clothes were strewn about the floor.

She kicked them into the corner, applied make-up with a jittery hand, and headed out.

The enormous white party tent was jammed with people. Men and women milled about drinking wine from stemmed glasses imprinted with, "Hawk and Winters" in black lettering.

Patty recognized a few faces, but most of the guests were not Clearwater regulars.

In the corner, a guitarist performed, *Summer of 69,* the ultimate song of reminiscence. His deep voice was rich and soulful.

She wavered. Empty wine glasses lined a table on one side of the tent. She could either go pick up a glass and search for Adam or slip out before he knew she'd been there. Heat rose up her neck, and her eye wanted to twitch. She didn't belong in this fancy, monied crowd.

"Patty."

Too late to escape

She straightened her shoulders and turned.

His crooked smile made her woozy.

"Hi," she said. "Great turn out."

"It is. I'm really pleased." Adam guided her toward a table laden with cheeses, crackers, bread sticks, dried fruits, dark red grapes, and dozens of votive candles. In the center were the cupcakes arranged on a three-tiered cupcake stand. "Do you like what I did with the cupcakes?"

"I love it. This table should be on the cover of a magazine," Patty said. "You're a man of many talents."

"That I am."

His innuendo stopped her.

Adam's face was flushed, his eyes dreamy. He took a chocolate cupcake, ate half of it, and offered her the other half.

Without thinking, she opened her mouth.

His thumb brushed against her lower lip. Chocolate and sweet frosting filled her mouth.

Adam handed her a glass of red wine. "Now, with my Syrah."

She sipped, and the tastes blended like colors in a sunset over the ocean. "Mmm, so good."

"I'm glad you came."

Patty's pulse pounded. "Me too."

"And you look great in that dress."

"Thank you."

"Hey, so." Adam shifted from foot to foot. "I wanted to say something about the other night."

She took a tremulous breath. "The other night?"

"Yeah, you know, the night I pulled your sister out of the bar?"

"Oh, yes, I do remember that." She reached for a glass of wine and took a drink. "You were quite the knight in shining armor." Patty drank more wine. At least she hadn't called him a Greek god to his face.

His expression was serious. “You asked about me and Kamila.”

“Did I?” She grabbed a chocolate cupcake and ate it in one bite.

“You wanted to know if we were getting back together.”

She grabbed a lemon cupcake and stuffed it into her mouth. “Really, truly, it’s none of my business.” Crumbs went flying.

“I want to be candid with you, Patty, because Kamila and I are—”

A distant voice interrupted him.

Adam looked past Patty. His face went from shock to anger in a split-second.

Kamila stumbled toward them. She had on white jeans, a red crop top, and platform sandals. Her hair cascaded over bare shoulders. “Hello, Adam,” she said, slurring her words. “You always did throw fabulous parties.”

Patty backed up.

“What are you doing here?” Adam demanded.

“It’s a party, isn’t it? And I do like parties.” She lurched forward, and he caught her arm.

“Oh, look who you’re with.” Kamila grinned. “I never thought you liked red heads, Adam.”

He moved between them. “You don’t belong here, Kamila. You weren’t invited.”

“I bought a ticket.” She snapped. “So I don’t need an invitation.”

Patty’s eye went twitchy. She *knew* she shouldn’t have come.

People noticed the conflict brewing and started whispering to one another.

Adam waved over one of the bartenders and handed Kamila off. “Take her home, Glen.”

Kamila twisted her shoulder like a child. “No, I don’t want to go.”

Glen the bartender practically lifted her off the ground and carried her out.

"I'll be right back." Adam followed the bartender and his ex out a side opening in the tent.

The guests returned to eating and drinking and dancing as if nothing happened.

Patty'd had enough. She'd been out of her mind to flirt with Adam. She had no business hanging around him or his rich friends.

Like a stealthy cat, she disappeared out the back of the tent and sprinted away.

The moon lit a path all the way up from the shore toward town, and stars shimmered against the black sky.

Patty slowed to catch her breath, annoyed with herself for going to the party in the first place.

She stopped when she heard footsteps pounding on the grass.

Adam practically knocked her over. "Hey, why'd you leave?"

"I—I need to get home."

"Come on, no you don't."

"Actually, I do."

"Are you leaving because of Kamila?"

Patty moved back, putting distance between them. It was way more than Kamila. "Why are you paying attention to me? Flirting with me and feeding me chocolate?"

His eyes widened. "I like you."

She liked him, too, but she wasn't about to say so. If she truly fell for him, no doubt she'd end up with a broken heart, and Patty had enough broken things to deal with.

The warm day had turned into a chilly night.

The scent of gunpowder hung in the air.

Adam stepped closer. "The answer is no. Kamila and I are not getting back together."

She wished they were.

Then she could deny her attraction and talk herself into believing she'd never actually liked him anyway.

It was obvious that being in the loft apartment had made him uncomfortable. In Patty's mind, that meant he wasn't over his ex.

"Seems to me," Patty said, choosing her words, "you're not exactly unencumbered. You may think you're not getting back together, but take it from me, a girl knows how to wriggle her way back in. And Kamila is one determined girl."

Adam laughed. "I assure you, Kamila has no interest in me. Not anymore. She just has to be the injured party."

She pressed her lips together, reserving judgement. In truth, she knew nothing about Kamila, except that she still wanted Adam, whether *he* knew it or not. "Don't you have to get back to your guests?"

"They'll be fine without me a few more minutes."

The night was dark, but a ray of moonlight illuminated Adam's profile.

He had a quiet strength about him, something she'd noticed with every encounter.

Patty ached for that kind of confidence—to have faith in herself, her decisions, her judgement. To be able to face challenges and crises without running away. How many times had she told herself to quit running?

Her compulsion to run was like drugs to an addict. The immediate relief of escape was irresistible, like floating away on a cool, blue sea of tranquility.

Her eye twitched, her hands shook, her heart raced. "Adam, I'm a mess. I have so many problems right now I can hardly keep them straight."

"Doesn't everyone?"

"I don't think so." She contemplated her siblings—Maggie with her rich husband and fancy new car; her brothers with their adoring wives and successful careers; and Liza—smart and sweet and beautiful—the girl who could be whatever she wanted.

He searched her face. "You know what I think? I think you're scared."

She bristled. Adam had touched a nerve. "Of course I am. Nothing, and I mean *nothing* in my life is on track. I live in limbo-land. I sleep in a storage room above a storeroom. I attract men who cheat on their wives. I had a freaking bathtub crash through my ceiling! If that's not a sign from above, I don't know what is."

He put his hands up in surrender. "Okay, stop, I get it. Boy, you are a handful, aren't you? Now, let me tell you a few things. I have my share of problems, but I deal with them. My life is pretty much on track, but I've worked my ass off to get it that way. There are plenty of men around who don't cheat, and if you attract men who do, that's on you. And just for the record, I've never cheated on a woman, nor would I. As for complications, there're always complications." Adam poked her shoulder. "And you, Patty Sullivan, are not all that complicated."

"Yeah, I am."

He shook his head. "No, you're not. I know what complicated is, and you're not it. And one more thing, you're tougher than you think you are."

Patty grabbed a tree trunk to steady herself, trying to comprehend his little speech. Was he so full of himself that he thought he understood her better than she understood herself?

Or was he right?

People didn't change overnight. But…she *had* been in Clearwater for two months, and two months wasn't overnight.

She straightened her back and lifted her chin. "Well, Adam, that was a mouthful. You've given me some things to think about."

"I'm glad."

"And so, I'm going to go back to my storage room apartment and think about them." She spoke deliberately without rambling. "Thank you for inviting me to the party. Goodnight."

Adam's chest rose and fell. "Fine. Goodnight."

With a quick nod, she whirled away. She forced herself to walk and not run.

"Patty, wait a sec."

Competing desires paralyzed her.

She wanted to run; she wanted to stay.

Adam closed the space between them. He turned her around and pulled her toward him.

His mouth melted into hers.

He tasted like wine and chocolate.

28

By morning, Patty had worked herself into a state of something between distress and panic.

Adam's kiss had been shocking, passionate—like Rhett Butler kissing Scarlett. It'd made her weak in the knees. Then, like Cinderella at midnight, she ran off. At least Cinderella had had a good reason.

At nine-fifteen, bright sunlight stabbed her eyes. She flew out of bed, threw on the red dress she'd left on the floor, and ran downstairs to find people waiting outside on the sidewalk.

"Oh crap." Patty unlocked the door and held it open. "Good morning, everyone. Welcome to Mariano's. I'll have samples out in just a minute."

She texted Liza.

Need you down here asap!

Two minutes later, her sister came in looking like she'd just rolled out of bed, because, in fact, she had.

The hustle and bustle lasted over an hour. When it finally quieted down, Patty made coffee. She watched it drip into the carafe. The aroma cleared her head.

Liza stood next to her and watched, too. "Is it ready?"

"Not yet. Hey, thanks for helping me out this morning."

"You're welcome. How was Adam's party?"

"Fine." She prepped two mugs with warmed milk and a sprinkle of raw sugar. She filled the mugs and handed one over.

They sipped at the same time, both holding their mugs in two hands. Her sister peered over the edge of her mug.

"What? You're looking at me funny."

"The party was fine? That's all you're going to say about it?"

"It was super nice. Lots of fancy wine and interesting people." Patty didn't see any point in elaborating.

Liza didn't know about her crush on Adam, and she wanted it to stay that way.

"Hey," Patty said. "Cupcake sales were fabulous yesterday. We sold out."

"I know. Everybody loved them." Her sister put her coffee mug on the counter. She glanced at the door. "Before anybody comes in, we need to talk about something."

Oh dear. Nothing good started with, '*we need to talk'*. "Okay. What is it?"

"Well, it's about, um, that I'm thinking, uh…"

"Liza, please just say it."

"I don't want to go back to Dallas tomorrow. I hate being in the house without Daddy. And ever since I took one stupid semester off, Mom and Maggie hover over me like they think I'm going to jump off a cliff. July is hot and miserable, all of my friends are in Europe or somewhere amazing, and—and I just don't want to go home yet!" She burst into tears.

Patty stepped back, surprised by the outburst, but not by her sister's wish to not go home. Everything she'd said was truc.

Besides, Liza had gone home every summer since her freshman year.

Patty had left home at eighteen and never visited for more than a week.

"Well." She summoned her big sisterly instincts. This was a chance to do better. "What do you want to do? Just hang out?"

"No." Her sister picked at her nail polish. "I talked to one of the bakers at Nutmeg's. She said I could, you know, be her assist…"

"So you already have it figured out?" Patty almost added, '*without talking to me?*' But why would she?

"Kind of," Liza said. She sounded almost apologetic, as if she were sorry to do be doing better than Patty.

At least that was how she heard it.

The door opened, and an older woman entered. "Hello, Patty."

She had no idea who the woman was. She smiled and masked her confusion "Hello, I'll be right with you." She put a hand on Liza's shoulder. "We'll talk more later. I have to get to work."

Liza sniffled. "Don't be mad at me, okay? I didn't plan this, not really."

Planned or not, it sounded like a done deal.

"We'll talk later," Patty said again.

"Okay." She nodded and left her alone with the strange but intriguing woman.

"So that's your sister. I could tell. You don't look much alike, except for your cute little noses, but I know a sisterly conversation when I hear it." The woman smiled. She had silver hair and deep wrinkles on her face. "It sounds to me like you're a good big sister."

Patty pursed her lips. How had the woman inferred that from only a few sentences? "Actually, I'm not."

The woman removed her sweater, a violet cardigan with tiny

pearl buttons. "If that's truly the case, my dear, it seems you've just been given the opportunity to change it."

Patty swayed.

The woman's words pushed against her like a strong wind. It was the same, or at least similar, advice Tessa and Cece and Julia had given her.

The wise counsel from her friends had floated around the edges of her awareness for weeks, ever since the night Liza had arrived.

Even though Patty had heard and understood their admonitions, it took the gentle nudge from this complete stranger for the truth to sink in.

Liza's appearance in Clearwater was not an intrusion.

It was a second chance.

29

Patty's eyes fixed on the old woman's face. Was she there to buy something, or had she entered Mariano's Cheese and Wine by divine intervention?

"Who are you?"

"My dear, I'm…"

In her mind, she heard, '*your fairy godmother.*' "I'm sorry, you're what?"

"Tessa's grandmother, Nonna."

Ah, it made perfect sense.

The wisdom of Tessa wrapped up in the body of a kind, gentle soul.

"Oh." She reached to shake her hand, but the woman pulled her into her arms. It was like falling onto angel food cake—sweet and soft, yet resilient. The hug didn't last long enough.

"I've heard all about you," Nonna said. "So, is Tessa here?"

Patty shook her head. "She's not coming in today."

The elderly woman folded her hands in front of her chin. "Oh, that's right. She told me last night about her headache, the poor dear. Well, this old brain doesn't work like it used to. I'll phone her later." She moved toward the door. "But if you talk to Tessa before I do, tell her I said she's doing the right thing."

"Okay."

What does that even mean?

"And." Nonna held up one finger, "remind her that the most important decisions we make in life are often the most difficult."

She blinked. Tessa's grandmother was Yoda with smaller ears and better skin.

"You won't forget my words, will you?"

Patty shook her head. "Never."

Nonna exited with a light wave, leaving her dumbfounded.

Afraid she might forget the exact words, she scribbled them on a napkin. Someday, she'd have them engraved in stone.

Fifteen minutes after Nonna left, Tessa showed up in sweats and flip-flops. Her hair was disheveled, her face pale. Large sunglasses covered her eyes.

Patty had never seen her look so awful. "What're you doing here?"

"I just need to check some inventory for the winetasting on Friday."

"Friday? I don't think I have it in the schedule."

"Oh, no." She removed her sunglasses and pinched her eyebrows together. "Did I forget to tell you? I've been so distracted."

"It's okay. I'll be here to help you. But are you going to be okay? Friday's only two days away."

"Yes. Absolutely."

Patty hoped that was true. "Oh, your grandmother came by. She left you a message." She gave her the napkin.

As Tessa read the words, the deep crease between her eyebrows softened. "Ah, Nonna, she always knows the right thing to say." The shop owner folded the napkin and started to put it in her purse.

"That's mine." Patty grabbed it. "I, um, I just wrote it down so I wouldn't forget. But I need to remember the words."

Tessa smiled softly. "Nonna got to you, did she?"

"I love her," Patty said. "And I don't mean like '*oh, I just love her'* because she's fun or funny or something. I mean I truly love her. I want her to be my Nonna, too."

"That's what everyone says." She ran a hand through her hair, making it look like she'd just come out of a wind tunnel. "Anyway, I'm just going to set aside some wines for Friday, then I'm going to the pharmacy, and home after that."

"Okay. Don't worry about anything here. I have it all under control." She stood taller. Nonna's words of wisdom had fortified her.

She was about to give Tessa a hug when the door swung open so violently the bells smacked the wall.

Kamila ran in, gasped for air like she'd just sprinted a mile. "Tessa, we have to talk."

The shop owner's face went from pale to a greenish white. "This isn't a good time. And besides, there's nothing to talk about. Your mother told me everything."

Patty moved behind the counter.

"I know. Please, let me explain."

"It won't change a thing, and I have to go."

Her cousin wouldn't be dissuaded. "It won't take long. I have to get this off my chest. You have no idea how horrible I feel."

"You feel horrible? I can't imagine why." The bitterness in her voice was fierce. "Maybe because I stood by you for five years, and now I look like a fool?"

The storm Patty had predicted was about to strike.

"I made a mistake," Kamila said. "A terrible mistake."

"A mistake?" Her brown eyes flashed. "Embezzling isn't a mistake. It's a felony. And you're lucky Adam didn't press charges! You could've landed in jail."

Patty slapped a hand over her mouth.

Embezzling?

So that's what led to the terrible breakup—not some sordid affair as she'd assumed.

"To make matters worse, you convinced me Adam had betrayed you."

"He did betray me." Her voice broke. "He banished me from my own home! He threatened to have me arrested if I didn't go into rehab."

"Of course he did! You stole from him! Jesus, Kamila, he loved you. Trusted you. Wanted to marry you. You made a fool out of him." She gripped the back of a chair. "I can't believe I let you manipulate me."

The vulnerability in her formidable friend shook Patty to her core.

"For five years, Adam kept your secret. At least your mother finally told me the truth, although she's suffering for it."

Tears pooled in Kamila eyes. "Not as much as I am," she whispered.

Silence took the air out of the room.

Tessa's face was ashen. "Why is it you always have to be the injured party?"

Patty reeled—*injured party*—Adam's exact words.

Kamila wrapped her arms around her stomach. She whimpered.

"You'd been clean for three years by that point. Everyone was in your corner, including Adam. Including *me*."

"I thought I could handle it," she said, her voice high and squeaky. "I didn't think it would get so bad again. But I'm sober now, I swear it."

Patty clenched her teeth. The drunken scene at Adam's party was less than a day ago.

"I'm starting over. Right this minute. And I need to tell you both how sorry I am."

Both?

The last thing Patty expected was to be drawn into somebody's twelve-step program.

Kamila reached across the counter and picked up her hand. "I'm terribly sorry, Patty. I was nasty, obnoxious, and rude. Will you forgive me?"

Patty drew her hand away. "Um, I guess so."

"Thank you." She sounded so sincere. She turned to her cousin.

"No." Tessa put her hands up "Don't ask me to forgive you again. You've been lying to me for years. For God's sake, you lied to me yesterday."

Huge tears fell from Kamila's beautiful eyes. "I know. I'm so sorry."

"All this time, I thought Adam had broken your heart, but it was you who broke his."

Patty was dizzy with the flood of information. Since her first encounter with Adam Hawk, she'd wanted to know more about him.

Now she knew more than she wanted.

Kamila hung her head, tears streaming down her cheeks. "I'm so sorry. Please, you have to forgive me."

Tessa recoiled, as if the apology scorched. Her expression hardened, and color returned to her skin. "No, Kamila, I don't have to forgive you."

Patty couldn't breathe. She felt their heartache as if it were her own.

Yet it was Kamila's pain that affected her most. How excruciating it must be to seek forgiveness, only to have it withheld.

30

As soon as Kamila left, Tessa locked the door and put out the closed sign. "I'm sorry you had to witness that, but now you know the whole story."

The truth was much worse than Patty had imagined.

"Is there anything I can do?"

"Nothing anybody can do now." The shop owner picked up her purse and left.

Patty cleaned the shop. She mopped the floor, polished the wood counters, dusted the shelves.

She rearranged cans, jars, packages, baskets, gifts, even the furniture in the tasting area. Maybe a fresh look would distract Tessa from her heartbreak.

Patty crossed the street and headed into the park, where a crew was removing red, white, and blue streamers from the gazebo.

Was the Fourth of July only yesterday?

Heat pressed on her shoulders as she followed a path without direction, preoccupied with troubles swirling around her like vultures.

A hot wind blew, carrying with it the smell of cinnamon.

She followed it to Nutmeg's, as if it were guiding her to her sister.

Inside the bakery, Trevor was wiping tables. "Hey, Patty, what'll you have?"

"Actually, nothing. I thought Liza might be here." A fresh tray of pecan sticky buns sat on the counter, steam rising.

"She was. Took off with Rebecca about half an hour ago." The barista made a little move with his shoulders. "I hear she's hanging out another few weeks."

"That's what I hear," Patty said, trying to sound chipper. "Anyway, I gotta run." The scent of toasted caramel pecans tugged at her. "Maybe a sticky bun to go. Charge it to my account."

"Oh, yeah, about your account," Trevor said, putting the pastry into a box. "You, um, you need to pay it."

"Did I forget to pay it?"

"You've never paid it." He opened a laptop and clicked on a spreadsheet—it had the names of practically every person who lived in Clearwater. "See? You started a tab back in May. Lattes and muffins and sticky buns add up."

"Oh my God." Her balance was almost two hundred dollars. "Did you send me a bill?"

He laughed. "We don't send bills. It's kinda the honor system. Hey, listen, don't worry about it. We know where to find you." Trevor handed her a little pink box.

Cha-ching.

Patty hesitated, but her hunger won out.

She sat at a round table on the outside patio under an umbrella. *Money, money, money.*

Most of every paycheck from Mariano's had gone toward her credit card balance. She hadn't looked at her bank account in ages.

Where did all her money go? Where was the check from the property manager?

Where was Liza?

The corner of her eye fluttered like a bird's wing. First things first. She called her sister. No answer.

Next up, checking account. She opened the app on her phone and tried to remember the password.

She had at least twenty, and they were scribbled on scraps of paper which she kept in various places. For a Millennial, she wasn't as tech savvy as she should be. Patty pressed on her temples. Were migraines contagious?

A black truck drove by. It slowed, stopped, and backed up.

The driver pulled into a parking space and the window went down.

"Oh my God."

Adam hitched an elbow over the frame. With the slightest motion of his head and a raised brow, he beckoned.

She rose to her feet, as if an invisible force had taken control of her.

"Want to go for a ride?" he asked.

Patty nodded.

"Don't forget your little bakery box there."

She retrieved her treat and got in.

They drove away from town and up a road to a rundown vineyard nestled in a thicket of trees.

He parked. Again, he motioned with his head. "Come on. And bring your snack with you."

She followed his instructions, her heart racing.

They walked toward a corral with a donkey and two horses.

Adam pulled carrots out of his back pocket. "Hello, ladies."

They munched and nuzzled his arm.

Each animal received one more.

"That's all I brought." He wiped his hands on his jeans and

headed into the brush, his big feet cutting a path in the overgrown weeds.

Patty followed him like a child skipping after the Pied Piper.

"Where are we?"

"Just a little farm. Friend of mine owns it, and we're fixing it up." He led her into a shady grove where a weathered wooden bench hung on thick ropes from a branch on a giant oak tree.

A gentle wind rustled the leaves, and their shadows danced on the ground. "It's beautiful here," Patty said.

Adam inhaled deeply. "It is, isn't it?"

They sat on the swing.

"What's in the box?" Amusement played on the corners of his smile.

"A sticky bun."

"A Clearwater favorite. I practically lived on those things in high school. It's how I grew into such a big strong boy."

"I'll bet." She opened the box, and tore a piece off. "Want some?"

"Sure." He winked and ate it out of her hand.

Patty squirmed. Last night she'd run from him like a nervous mouse. Now, she wanted to climb into his lap.

The last twenty-four hours, especially the horrible confrontation between Tessa and Kamila, had exhausted her. She smoothed the skirt on her red dress.

"Did you sleep in your clothes?"

"Oh, um…" She laughed. "I might as well have."

"It looked great on you last night, and it still does. You should wear it every day."

The man was a master at charm. He'd turned embarrassment into flattery.

"What are we doing, Adam?"

"We're talking. And eating a sticky bun." He broke off another piece and ate it, licking his thumb. "At least I am."

He was toying with her.

Patty put her hand on his chest, as if holding him at bay, and felt his muscles through the thin fabric of his shirt. "I think I like you more than I should."

"More than you should?"

She tried to clear her fuzzy head, sorry she'd said it. "Why are we here?"

He drew back. "Well, I'd like to talk. You took off pretty fast last night."

She looked down at her hands. "I know. I'm sorry."

"You don't need to apologize. That scene with Kamila put everyone a little on edge."

The memory of his ex-girlfriend's confession weighed heavily on Patty. "There's something I need to tell you."

"So tell me."

"I know about Kamila."

"Of course you do." He rocked the swing. "You were there."

"No, I mean *all* about Kamila." She twisted her hands. "The rehab, the embezzling, you threatening to press charges if she didn't leave town."

His gray-blue eyes met hers. "How do you know about that?"

Patty told him what she'd witnessed that morning, worried he might get mad.

"Huh," he said. "Kamila came clean. That is progress."

The non-reaction surprised her. "So it's true? Even the part about you threatening to press charges?"

Adam nodded. "I did her a favor. If I hadn't made her leave Clearwater, she'd have ended up doing far worse."

"Worse than embezzling?"

"You ever watch *Law and Order*?"

"I love that show, especially the old ones."

He perked up. "Yeah? Me, too. Anyway, Kamila was headed in that direction. And believe me, she wouldn't look good in an orange jumpsuit."

"Oh my God." Patty put a hand on her chest. He wasn't kidding about knowing what complicated was.

"I can't blame her for wanting to have a little fun. We were young, I was working non-stop, and she found a group of friends in Oakland." He inhaled and shook his head. "But they were into all kinds of, you know, stuff. By the time I realized what was going on, she was already in major trouble. Sophia and I untangled it and got her the hell out of here. Nobody knew except for us—until now."

The conversation had turned decidedly unromantic.

He rubbed the scruff on his chin. "Anyway, that's why I told Tessa not to hire her. I mean, an addict working in a wine shop? That's almost as insane as an addict marrying a winemaker."

Patty twisted her moon charm between her fingers. Kamila's distressed face haunted her. "I guess so."

Adam pointed at the sticky bun. One side of his mouth lifted. "Can I have more?"

"Sure." She gave him the box.

He took a big bite. A bit of gooey caramel stuck to his lower lip and he licked with the tip of his tongue. "I didn't bring you here to talk about my ex-girlfriend. I want to talk about last night. About us."

The seat felt hard underneath Patty's bottom. She shifted. "Listen, after hearing your story, I know my situation's uncomplicated to you, but it isn't to me. I'm drowning in craziness. My home's about to be flattened. My sister's still here, and something's up with her. And now poor Tessa's a wreck. I mean, the Kamila news has devastated her."

"I know. They're very close. At least they were."

Patty continued unloading. "I love Tessa. I admire her. But she's tough sometimes. And impossible to figure out."

"That's a Mariano woman for you." He wiped his mouth with the back of his hand. "They say what they think most of the time, but then they hold back. You never know what's going to happen next."

"Exactly! And boy oh boy, is she secretive. What about those cases of wine she ordered? She told me Hawk and Winters wines would never stand on her shelves, and then out of the blue they show up."

Adam's eyebrows slanted toward his nose. "What're you talking about?"

Patty covered her mouth.

"Tessa ordered my wine?"

She clenched her teeth.

"Where'd it come from?" He cocked his head like a curious dog. "We deliver ourselves around here. And believe me, if an order had been placed by Mariano's, I would've noticed."

"UPS." She pressed the corner of her eye but not in time. The twitch started up.

"No, I mean the distributor."

Just like that, he was all business. He pulled out his phone and started typing. "I wonder if it came through Reno."

She sat there with her mouth open. The sudden change in his demeanor was fascinating.

Adam stood, still typing, and walked toward his truck.

Patty followed.

He leaned on the door, continuing to type. Then he stopped and looked up. "Are you free tomorrow night?"

"What?"

"I want to take you to dinner."

"You mean you're not mad about the wine?"

"Mad? I'm thrilled. If Tessa's lightening up on her boycott of my wines, this could be huge for me. She's one of the most influential wine sellers in the region. This is a game-changer." He tossed his phone through the window onto the driver's seat. "So, will you go to dinner with me?"

"You mean like a date?"

"Yeah," Adam said, stretching out the word. "You know, I pick you up, I drive to a restaurant, we eat dinner, I pay the bill, we leave the restaurant, take a walk, kiss in the moonlight. Stuff like that." His eyebrows waggled expectantly, waiting for her answer.

Patty folded her arms. "Are you teasing me?"

He licked his lips. "Absolutely not."

"Okay." Her legs melted into jelly. "I'll go to dinner with you."

And kiss you in the moonlight.

"Great. I'll let you know the plan tomorrow." He opened the door to his truck.

"Wait. You're leaving me here?"

"Oh, yeah, sorry. Where are you headed?"

Where am I headed?

"I was, uh, I'm going to Cece's house."

"Perfect." Adam pointed over her shoulder. "It's right over there."

"It is?" She saw nothing but trees. "Where?"

"Beyond those bushes. Go straight past the corral and you'll come out on their street. About a five-minute walk. It'd take us longer to drive there."

"Okay."

"You want me to walk with you?"

She liked the offer, but he obviously had business to attend to. "I think I can handle it."

Adam winked. "I'm sure of it."

31

"Cece!" She blew in through the front door. "Where are you?"

"Shhh!" Her friend came running from the kitchen. "Noah's napping."

"I need to talk to you." Patty tried to catch her breath.

"You sure do."

"What's wrong?" She followed Cece into the kitchen and halted.

Her little sister sat at the kitchen table with Shadow in her lap. Her eyes were red-rimmed.

"Liza, I was looking for you. What're you doing here?"

"I just came by to bring Cece some cookies I made." She pointed at the familiar Nutmeg's box.

"I wanted to finish our conversation from this morning. You know, about you staying and working at Nutmeg's."

Liza nudged the cat off her lap and stood. "Can we talk later? I'm meeting Rebecca. She invited me over for dinner."

"Oh. Okay, sure." She looked at the clock on the microwave, surprised to see how late it was. "I'll see you later then."

"Right," her sister said, moving quickly toward the door. "Bye Cece, and, um, thanks."

As soon as the door closed, Patty reacted. "Why was Liza here? Why was she crying? What'd she want?"

"Take it easy." Cece opened the refrigerator. "Do you want to eat leftovers with me? Brad's at a meeting tonight."

"Yes, I do. And I'd like glass of wine."

"Help yourself."

"Fine. I will." Patty scanned the selection in the wine rack. A Malbec from a winery in Carmel caught her eye. They carried it at Mariano's, but she'd never tasted it. "Okay if we open this one?"

"Is it tagged?"

"No."

Special occasion bottles were marked.

"Then yes."

The tension between them baffled Patty. "Are we mad at each other?"

"Well," Cece said. "Are you mad at *me*?"

"I wasn't. But if you're mad at me, then yes. I came here with big news, and now I've practically forgotten what it was."

Her friend put two wine glasses on the island. "Talk fast, because Noah will be waking up any minute."

"You first. What did Liza want?"

"No, you first. What's the big news?"

"Adam asked me out."

Cece's eyes went wide. "On a date?"

Patty nodded. "That's what he said."

She recalled Adam's description of what a date would him entail, including kissing in the moonlight.

"And you said yes, didn't you?"

"I did." Patty poured the wine. "But we'll get back to that in a minute. Why was my sister here?"

Cece twisted her mouth. "Liza is, well, you kind of hurt her feelings."

"She's so sensitive," Patty said. "And she has her period."

"That may be, but she you reacted badly to her plan to stay longer."

Patty sat on a stool and leaned on her elbows. "All I said was that we'd talk about it later. Geez, it's not like I was surprised. She's been putting off going home since the day she got here."

"That's true." Her friend sat next to her.

Patty sipped the wine. Held it in her mouth before swallowing. Dark berries, peppery notes. *Excellent.* "Taste the wine, tell me what you think."

Cece shook her head. "How is it you have so much going on in that brain of yours? We're talking about Liza, not wine."

"I've become very good at multi-tasking." She moved her hands like a juggler. "I picked it up from Tessa."

Another memory from the day popped into Patty's head, the blow-up between Tessa and Kamila. She pushed it into a back corner.

"Let's focus on Liza," her friend said. "She thinks you're mad at her. Are you?"

Patty tried to recall the conversation. "Not mad, exactly. Maybe a little frustrated. But then I talked to Nonna."

"Nonna?"

"Tessa's grandmother. She's like a wise sage."

"A wise sage? Really?"

"Yes." She prepared herself to recite the words. "Nonna said, '*the most important decisions we make are often the most difficult'*."

"Sorry, but that's just common sense."

Patty pouted. "It sounded better when Nonna said it. Anyway, she made me realize I could be a better sister."

"What an epiphany—I've been telling you that for a month."

"I know. It's just taking a while for it to sink in."

Cece *tsk-tsked.* "I'll say." She took a large shortbread cookie out of the box Liza had brought and broke it in half.

Patty ate a piece. It was crisp and buttery with a hint of citrus. "Oh wow. So good."

Cece licked crumbs off her lips. "This might be the best cookie I've ever eaten." She closed the box. "We'll save the rest for later. Now, after dinner, you'll go back to the loft and talk it out with Liza. Then you'll look at your clothes and figure out what to wear tomorrow night."

Tomorrow night. Dinner with Adam.

Her stomach fluttered like a butterfly caught in a net.

It was dark when Patty returned to the loft. She flipped on a light. "Liza, where are you?" She knocked on the bathroom door as she opened it.

There was a note taped to the mirror.

Patty, I never meant to cause you any trouble. Sorry if I did. I'm going to stay with Rebecca.

Love, Liza

She stared at the note, reading it over and over.

Once again, she had let her little sister down.

32

Over the next twenty-four hours, Patty tried to reach Liza. Her calls and texts went unanswered.

Finally, her sister responded.

Don't worry I'm fine talk tomorrow, K? xoxo

"Okay then." Patty replied with a thumbs up and smiley face emoji.

With Liza off her worry-list for the time being, she searched for her favorite boots. She tossed everything out of the closet and found one of the trash bags Captain Brandt had given her to pack in.

She turned it upside down. Out came belts, socks, winter sweaters, and a pair of leggings she'd forgotten she had. Patty gave the bag another shake, and her red cowboy boots hit the floor. What a relief—they'd cost half a month's rent.

In gray skinny jeans, a sleeveless black top, and her red boots, Patty headed downstairs.

Through the glass door, she saw Adam standing on the sidewalk beside his black truck. It was a magazine photo waiting to be taken.

Her stomach flip-flopped like a teenager's on prom night.

She opened the door. "Hi."

He wore dark jeans and a pale blue shirt with the sleeves rolled up. His beard, usually bushy, had been trimmed close, accentuating a strong jaw.

"Hi," Adam said. "You look great."

"Tha—" her voice squeaked. "Thanks. You do, too."

He opened the passenger door and helped her step up into the cab.

As he walked around to the driver's side, she checked her face in the mirror. "Pull yourself together," she whispered to her reflection.

Adam hopped into the driver's seat. "You're gonna like where we're going."

"How do you know?" she teased.

He put an arm around her shoulders. "Because I know what you like." He pulled her closer, and the woody scent of his cologne emanated off his skin.

His kiss was light, like a quick hello, but it made her shiver, and a small sigh escaped her lips.

Adam drew back and smiled.

Oh, that smile.

"Those," he said, pointing to her feet, "are great boots."

They drove south.

The acres of open land and vineyards gave way to suburbs and neighborhoods and strip centers with big box stores.

"Are we going to San Francisco?" She hadn't been out of Clearwater since the day she'd arrived on Cece's doorstep.

"We certainly are."

From the Golden Gate Bridge, Patty looked into the bay. The

sun shimmered on the water, and the sky was a canvas of orange, pink, and blue.

"This view never gets old," he said.

She'd driven across the bridge dozens of times over the years, but with Adam sitting beside her, she had a new appreciation for it.

Once in the city, the traffic slowed.

Their conversation lagged. Patty got jittery, and her knees bounced. Then her eye twitched a tiny bit, making her even more anxious.

"I'm taking you to my favorite Italian restaurant."

The words rescued her, and she relaxed. She could talk about food for hours. "Sounds wonderful, and I'm starving."

"Good. We're almost there." He turned into an alley and parked the truck behind a restaurant, blocking a big Mercedes.

"I don't think you can park here."

"Don't worry." Adam flashed a sly grin. "I assure you, I can."

The power he exuded roused Patty. Never had she known a man so in control and confident, let alone one with a crooked smile that gave her goosebumps.

He took her hand and guided her into the bustling kitchen.

The smell of sautéed garlic and fresh baked bread made Patty salivate.

A burly man in a white chef's jacket greeted Adam with a man-hug, slapping him hard on the back. "Where you been, my friend?" The chef had black and gray hair and a charming Italian accent. He turned to her and picked up her hand. "And who is this? *Una bella regazza*!"

Patty had no idea what *bella regazza* meant, but her knees went wobbly.

Adam wrapped an arm around her waist and introduced her. "Lorenzo put Hawk and Winters on the map. If not for him, I'd still be peddling my wines around Sonoma in a little red wagon."

Lorenzo laughed heartily. "No, no, my friend. You make excellent wine, I buy excellent wine. That is what is business. Good business and good friendship. Now, follow me."

Patty looked Adam as they walked. "Are you trying to impress me?"

"Yes. Is it working?"

She batted her eyelashes. "Oh, you have no idea."

They were seated at a corner table under a low-hanging fixture that cast warm yellow light on the white table cloth.

"This is beautiful." She smoothed the cloth napkin in her lap.

A waiter appeared with sparkling water, two glasses of red wine, an assortment of appetizers, and a round baguette. He placed them on the table and disappeared.

"These," Adam said, "are balsamic roasted figs wrapped in prosciutto." He lifted the plate and she took one.

The flavors blended in her mouth, sweet and savory. "Oh wow, I've never tasted anything like that."

He ate one and let out a little moan. Then he broke the baguette and handed her a small piece. "A bite of bread, and then we'll try the wine."

Patty followed his instructions. The bread was warm, crusty on the outside, moist and dense and buttery in the middle.

Adam raised his glass of wine.

She lifted hers. "Hawk and Winters?"

"Actually, no." He tapped his glass to hers. "This is one of Lorenzo's. He's from a little town in Northern Italy. His family's winery has been there for generations."

They tasted.

She held the wine in her mouth for a moment, allowing it to linger. Then closed her eyes and swallowed. "It's… it's like drinking velvet."

"Wow, I'm impressed. Your palate has become quite sophisticated."

As they drank, more food appeared on small plates. "Lorenzo's making a special menu for us. He wants us to try all his specialties."

They shared everything—bigoli pasta with red wine and roasted duck sauce, tortellini floating in a shallow pool of homemade chicken broth, clams and mussels in a spicy tomato sauce.

"Mmm," Patty said with her mouth full. She broke off a piece of bread and soaked it in the broth. She put it in her mouth and licked her fingers. "Oh, geez." She wiped a drip of broth off her chin with the back of her hand. "Where are my manners?"

"With food like this, it's appropriate to eat with your fingers." Adam's eyes stayed with hers as they drank more wine.

Although the restaurant was noisy and packed, she didn't notice anybody other than him.

Only the two of them occupied her space and awareness.

She drenched another piece of bread in the spicy tomato sauce. Marinara trickled down her thumb to her wrist. "I have to admit, I do like eating with my fingers."

"I do, too." Adam pulled her hand toward him and licked the sauce from her skin with the tip of his tongue. He took the bread into his mouth and closed his lips around her fingers.

The sensation set off sparks inside her.

It didn't stop. More wine. More food. More delicious kisses.

Patty fell under his spell.

Dessert arrived. A sliver of chocolate torte with a dusting of powdered sugar.

"I can't eat another thing. Please don't make me."

"I'd never do that." He took a bite of the cake and closed his eyes as he swallowed.

"Is it good?"

"No. You wouldn't like it."

"You just want it all for yourself, don't you?"

Adam took another bite. "Maybe."

Patty pushed her fork into the cake. "One teeny bite. That's all I'm gonna have."

The cake had a thin crispness on top, moist and rich in the middle. It dissolved in her mouth.

He lifted her chin with two fingers. "You have a tiny bit of chocolate…" he licked her upper lip, "right there."

His kiss took her breath away.

A warm hand slipped under her shirt and caressed the small of her back.

She held his face and kissed his mouth with abandon.

Every thought and care and worry left Patty's mind.

Adam took up all of it, leaving no room for anyone or anything else.

33

Adam kept glancing at Patty as he drove, as if making sure she was still there.

"Why do you keep looking at me?" She flashed a flirtatious smile.

"You're so pretty. I can't help myself."

Pretty? The only man who'd ever thought she was pretty was her father. "So you have a thing for tiny girls with crazy red hair?"

"No." He grinned and put a hand on her leg. "I have a thing for *this* tiny girl with crazy red hair."

Patty chewed on her lower lip. She waited for her eye to twitch, but it didn't.

Clearwater came into view, a yellow moon lighting up the road. Adam slowed his truck. "Would you like to come back to my place?"

She gulped. "Well, um, okay."

Ten minutes later, they turned on the dark road that led into the Hawk family vineyard.

Patty struggled to keep her breathing steady.

As if sensing her trepidation, he enfolded her hand inside of his. "Relax. I'm not expecting anything. I just want to be with you a little longer."

How did he always know the right thing to say?

A pleasing warmth filled her down to her toes.

The house came into view, but she hardly noticed. She was too preoccupied gazing at Adam's profile.

"Holy shit." He slammed on the brakes.

Patty bounced forward and back.

On the porch, a figure dressed in black faced the door. The truck rolled closer, tires crunching on the gravel, and the person turned.

"It's Kamila," Adam said.

She looked like a cat burglar, a very attractive cat burglar. With the headlights shining into her face, Kamila shielded her eyes.

He parked in front of the porch and opened his door. "Stay here. This won't take long."

Before Patty could respond, he was walking up the steps toward his ex-fiance.

Kamila's distraught face in the shadowy light was haunting.

Adam stopped in front of her, his back to Patty, and put his hands on his hips.

She started talking, her arms around her own waist.

Patty opened the door a crack to hear what she was saying. The wind carried the conversation in the other direction.

All she had to work with were facial expressions and body language. Not much to go on. Then Kamila wrapped her arms around Adam's neck.

He took her wrists and lowered her arms to her sides, but she persisted.

He backed up, and she moved forward, giving Patty a clearer view.

Tessa's cousin, his ex-fiance, kept talking.

Adam shook his head.

Kamila's shoulders heaved up and down.

Then he took her in his arms and held her.

Patty didn't need to see more.

No matter what happened next, her date with Adam was over.

She slipped out of the truck and tiptoed down the driveway.

Once she got to the road, she leaned against a tree, pulled off her boots, and sprinted away, hoping she'd get far enough so he couldn't find her. Because as soon as he realized she'd left, he'd go looking for her.

He was that kind of man—responsible, caring, chivalrous.

No wonder Kamila had come back for him.

On bare feet, she ran until a sharp rock stabbed her heel. "Owww!" Her eyes burned, and a wave of self-pity washed over her.

Winded and in pain, she texted Cece.

Sorry it's so late. U up?

An immediate response: *Yes! How was date?*

I'm stranded can you come get me?

Where are you?

I don't know somewhere near Adam's house.

Stay put I'll track your phone

. . .

She backed up into a thick of trees to wait.

The best date of her life had turned into the worst.

Adam might be the man of her dreams, but their attempt at romance was a nightmare. They both just had too much baggage.

An owl hooted, or at least it sounded like an owl. Maybe it was a wolf. Were there wolves in wine country?

She pictured a pack of them howling at the moon.

The sound of a car coming in her direction caught her attention.

Patty ran toward the road to wave Cece down. "Oh no!"

Adam's truck approached at slow speed.

She scrambled back into the bushes, tripped, and went down face first into the dirt. Her boots and cellphone flew out of her hands. "Youch!" Whimpering like a hurt puppy, she got onto her knees and crawled through the brush to find her phone.

What a stupid idea it was to sneak out of the truck and scurry away. Her date might've been ruined, but at least she would've had a ride home.

Instead, she was creeping around in the dark like a prison escapee. Her hand hit one boot, and she tucked it under her arm. Then she found her phone and turned on the flashlight. The light beam landed on two huge, round black eyes.

Patty shrieked.

The masked animal bared its teeth. It lunged at her with sharp claws and a ferocious growl.

She flung herself in the other direction, tumbling into a mud puddle, soaking her clothes, and scraping her arm. Terrified, she rolled over and over until she hit the pavement with her cheekbone. The abrasion burned like a dozen bee stings.

Patty jumped to her feet and took off running. Headlights came toward her. She hoped it was Cece, but by this point she'd have gotten into a car with anybody.

The car passed by, made a U-turn, and pulled up beside her.

She yanked open the door. "Thank God it's you." She dove in like a bank robber jumping into a getaway car.

Cece, wearing pajamas and flip-flops, gasped. "What happened? You're a mess!"

She wiped mud and blood from her cheek. She had dirt in her mouth. "I'll tell you, just drive."

Her friend hit the gas. "Are you in trouble? Did you break the law?"

"I wish it were that simple."

As Cece drove, she told her everything, including and up to the horrifying racoon attack. "It was the best night ever until it turned into the worst."

Her friend grimaced. "What a disaster."

Patty dragged a muddy sleeve across her face. "And I lost one of my boots. I'll bet that racoon ran off with it like a trophy."

"Yeah, racoons do steal things—I saw it on YouTube."

She wanted to wail like a baby. Her cheek smarted, the heels of both hands were embedded with bits of gravel, she'd ripped a hole in the knee of her jeans, and she'd lost a boot—a very expensive one.

"I'm taking you to my house," Cece said with authority.

Patty sniffled and shook her head. "No. Just drop me off at the loft."

"Are you sure? I don't think you should be alone."

"I'll be fine." All she wanted to do was go to bed.

Her friend parked in front of Mariano's. "Do you need me to come up with you?"

She shook her head.

Cece's face was full of concern. "I'll call you in the morning, okay?"

"Yeah." Patty opened the door. "Thanks for rescuing me." She yelped when her injured toe hit the curb.

"Are you sure you're all right?"

"I'll know more after I peel off these clothes and check my bruises." She got out of the car. "Talk to you tomorrow."

The warmth of the shop and the scent of spices and wood comforted her. She plodded up the stairs, one hand on the banister and the other clutching her boot. She opened the door to another surprise—Liza asleep on her bed.

As if the night hadn't been crazy enough already.

Patty looked down at her.

Her sister held her phone as if she'd fallen asleep in the middle of a call.

She slipped it out of her relaxed hand, and the screen saver came to life. "Oh, wow."

It was an old photo of them in their backyard. Liza couldn't have been more than three. They were sitting in the grass having a tea party, both of them sipping from plastic tea cups. Her little sister was looking up at her with adoration, and Patty was leaning toward her, their noses touching.

The image brought back a memory long forgotten. Patty's chest tightened. So many regrets, mistakes, and missed opportunities.

The phone vibrated, and she jumped. Who would be texting at this hour? She gasped.

The text was from Maggie. Of course, the sister who didn't sleep.

Patty scrolled through and found a stream of messages that had come in over the last few hours.

Liza call me!

Liza, why aren't you calling me back?

. . .

Liza, Mom said you're not answering her calls and now you're not answering mine!

Come on Liza, what is going on with you?

She jiggled her sister's shoulder. What had she done that sent their big sister over the edge? "Liza, wake up."

Her sister mumbled and turned over. She'd always been a heavy sleeper.

She had three options—dump cold water on Liza's face, rip apart all of Liza's belongings in search of clues, or take a shower and go to bed.

Patty opted for the shower and bed. Whatever was going on between Maggie and Liza could wait until morning. She'd had enough stress for one night.

In the tiny bathroom, she removed her muddy clothes and examined her bumps and bruises.

The abrasion on her cheek had bits of dirt in it. She looked like she'd been in a fight, a fight with a thieving racoon who stole her boot.

Patty turned the water as hot as she could stand it. It stung her skin.

Her ego stung even more.

34

Despite her traumatic night, Patty fell asleep and stayed asleep until her alarm screeched at eight. She tumbled off the blow-up mattress and hit the floor. "Ouch!"

She looked up to see her bed neatly made and a yellow sticky note stuck to the nightstand.

Couldn't stay at Rebecca's. Will explain later.

Patty crunched up the note. No mention of Maggie. Maybe there wasn't some huge problem. Their older sister tended to overreact —her demanding texts were probably a big to-do about nothing. Or so she hoped.

She wouldn't investigate any further. Steering clear of whatever the issue was between her two sisters was the smart way to go. She got to her feet and went to the bathroom to assess her injuries.

The worst was her cheek. The gash had turned red and

purple, and make-up only made it look worse. She gave up, got herself dressed, and headed downstairs.

In need of a caffeine jolt, Patty made a double espresso. She watched it drip into a tiny cup. Her body ached, her cheek stung, her arm burned.

Most of all, she was crushed to have lost her boot.

She dumped two packets of sugar into her coffee and knocked it back. Her cellphone vibrated in her pocket. She pulled it out, expecting Cece.

It was Adam.

Patty stared at the screen until the buzzing stopped. Better to let him leave a message. At least then she'd have an idea of what his reaction was to her running away. He might be mad.

Probably not.

He might be apologetic

Possibly.

Or he might think she was a crazy nutcase for slinking away without a word and disappearing into the night.

Most likely.

A few customers came in and browsed, as if they had all the time in the world.

Patty's hands shook from too much caffeine and stress.

She tried to put Adam and Liza out of her mind, but both refused to leave.

Once the customers finished browsing, and not buying, she scribbled a note saying she'd be back in ten minutes, taped it to the door, and dashed over to Nutmeg's.

Time to meet one of her worries head on.

Mid-morning sunlight sparkled on the sidewalk. With each step, Patty's bruised foot reminded her of how her date with Adam had ended.

Inside Nutmeg's, she went around the counter and let herself into the kitchen. It smelled like yeast and cinnamon and toasted nuts.

Her little sister did a double take. "What happened to your face?"

Patty touched her cheek where it'd hit the pavement. It smarted. "It's nothing, just a scrape."

Liza took a closer look. "It's not nothing."

She ignored her sister's concern and moved on to more pressing matters. "So what happened to staying with Rebecca?"

"Oh, well, it just didn't work out." She sifted flour into a measuring cup. "Sorry I fell asleep in your bed."

"It's okay." They eyed each other.

Her sister was hiding something, and her curiosity about Maggie's texts wormed its way in, pushing aside her sensible decision to stay out of it. "Why was Maggie texting you last night? She sounded frantic."

"I figured you'd read my texts."

"I couldn't help it. Your phone buzzed in my hand." Patty defended her snooping. As much as she wanted to avoid conflict and drama, she was curious—and concerned.

"Don't worry about it." She cracked eggs into a bowl with one hand. "Maggie's just trying to manage everything. It's how she is, you know that."

Patty did. Still, she couldn't shake the feeling that there was more to the story.

Liza wiped her hands on a towel. "I'm sorry about the other day, you know, when I went to talk to Cece."

"You don't need to apologize." She unwound a little. "You're free to visit anybody you want. Anyway, I just came to make sure everything was okay with you and Maggie."

"Yeah, it's all fine." Her sister stirred the mixture. "So, where were you last night?"

"Me?"

Liza arched an eyebrow. "Yeah, you."

"Oh, uh, I was with Cece. She dropped me off late." It was

the truth, sort of. "I gotta get back to the shop. See you later." Patty dashed out the door before her sister could ask any more questions.

~

A few hours later, another game changer.

Patty had just sold a case of expensive wine and was quite pleased with herself when Tessa facetimed her. She answered right away. "Hi."

"Hi—oh my god, what happened to you?"

She grimaced. She'd forgotten about her face. "It's nothing, just a scrape. Hey, I have good news."

"I could use some good news." Tessa rubbed her temples.

"We just sold a whole case of that French Bordeaux."

Her squinty eyes opened a little. "No kidding. That's great."

"Yeah, I know. The guy was in here forever, asking a million questions, but it was worth it."

"Thank you." She smiled, although it looked as if it hurt her to do so.

"How's your headache?"

"Not good. It started to get better, but then last night it got worse again." Tessa put on her sunglasses, even though she was in her kitchen. "I can't make it to the winetasting tonight."

Patty stared at her phone. "Oh, that's bad. I mean, it sounds like a high-end crowd. And I'm no sommelier."

"Don't worry, you're still just assisting. I got Adam to run it."

Her blood pressure dropped. Or maybe it skyrocketed. It was hard to tell. "Adam?"

"I was going to cancel, then I remembered we're featuring several Hawk and Winters wines. So I called Adam, and he couldn't have been more gracious."

Gracious.

That sounded like him.

"Wonderful." She choked on the word.

35

The thought of seeing Adam, let alone assisting him, had her stomach in knots. Never-the-less, despite the debacle of the prior night, she was determined to appear professional and composed.

Patty dressed in black jeans and a conservative white cotton shirt. Thankfully, the scrape on her cheek had faded to pink.

She dabbed it with concealer and blew her hair forward. As long as nobody looked at her too closely, they wouldn't notice it. Or so she hoped. To distract, she put on a pair of colorful feather earrings.

Adam arrived only fifteen minutes before the tasting. When he walked into the shop, her breath caught. In khaki pants, a white dress shirt, and a tie the same color as his eyes, he was more handsome than ever.

She stood behind the counter, trying to hide her scraped cheek. Patty forgot all about her face when he handed her a red boot.

"Oh my God, where'd you find it?" She clutched it to her chest like a lost kitten.

"On the side of the road just past my house." He pointed at her cheek. "What happened there?"

She put a hand over the scrape. "It's a long story."

"Something to do with the lost boot?"

"Kinda." Patty pulled more hair forward. "Thank you for finding it."

"You're welcome." Adam checked his watch. "I gotta go get some wine out of my truck."

"Okay." She tried to match Adam's frosty tone. It wasn't her fault Kamila had shown up and ruined their date.

On the other hand, she'd performed her Cinderella act once again. She'd even left the shoe behind.

While he was outside, she smoothed the white cloth on the long table which she had set with wine glasses, decanters, black cocktail napkins, and small plates.

In the center was a charcuterie tray laden with cheese, crackers, prosciutto, Marcona almonds, olives, and dried fruit. She admired her work. Tessa would be pleased with the display, too.

Adam returned with a box in his arms and Tipsy at his heels.

The dog jumped in the air as if Patty were his favorite person in the world.

She caught him mid-jump. "Hello, Tipsy."

He licked her face.

"He sure likes you." Adam's tone had warmed up a little.

"I like him, too." She put the dog down and watched Adam arrange the wine.

His sleeves were rolled up to his elbows, the grapevine tattoo visible.

"Did you make this?" He pointed to the tray.

Patty nodded.

"Nice selection." He tasted a piece of cheese, savoring it as if analyzing the flavor. "Mmm, Manchego, right?"

She nodded. "It'll go well with the Syrah."

A corner of his mouth curved up. "Yes, it will."

She was about to say something about her mad dash down his driveway last night when the bells on the door jingled and six men walked in.

They were laughing and slapping each other on the shoulders. Maybe they weren't such a high-end bunch after all, just a group out to have fun rather than an audience truly interested in the intricacies of wine.

Six weeks ago, Patty wouldn't have known the difference. But now she did. "Looks like party night. What a waste of our time."

Adam pulled a cork from one of the bottles. "Tastings are never a waste of time."

"Really?" she lowered her voice. "You think any one of these guys really cares about wine?"

"Maybe, maybe not. But it doesn't matter, Patty. Wine making is an art. And wine selling is a business." He waved the men over. "And I'm good at both."

As it turned out, the men were captivated by his knowledge. They also had plenty of money. With every pour, they ordered more wine.

Adam blended in with them as if he were one of the guys. He complimented them on their discerning tastes, laughed at their jokes, and returned their high-fives.

Patty faded into the background. She kept the snacks filled, replaced glasses as needed, and noticed how expertly he fit into any crowd.

The event wound down, and she picked up the order sheets.

Most of the men bought several cases, amounting to a lucrative night for Mariano's, as well as for Adam.

She organized the purchases on the counter near the register and stood by waiting to ring up sales.

One of the men came over to her. He had black hair and smooth, tanned skin. "I need a few gifts," he said. "Can you help me pick some things out?"

"Sure." Patty came around the counter, happy to put her expertise to good use. "Did you have anything special in mind? Sweet, savory, spicy?"

"Whatever you recommend. I'm Dennis, by the way." He extended a hand for a shake.

"Patty." She glanced in Adam's direction, but he was busy schmoozing with the guests. "Over here we have a fabulous selection of herbs and spices. My favorite is this grilling rub."

"I love a good rub." Dennis gave her a suggestive smile.

She opened the sample jar for him to take a whiff.

"Oh, wow. Amazing. I'll take a dozen."

A dozen?

She did the math in her head and guided him to another display. "These are homemade relishes. They're delicious and really—"

Dennis touched her lower back.

"Yes?" he asked without moving his hand.

Patty stepped away with a surreptitious glide. "Relishes are great with chicken and meats of all kinds."

"I can tell you have good taste, so you pick out whatever you like best." Dennis grinned, his teeth shiny white. "I'm sure I'll be pleased."

"Okay." She returned the smile and selected a variety of relishes, chutneys, three kinds of olive tapenade. On a whim, she threw in a tin of pricy caviar.

They carried his items to the register.

Dennis watched her ring up his purchase. He leaned on the counter with a casual tip of the head. "Those are great earrings, by the way."

"Thank you." Patty focused on the barcodes.

"So, you live in this charming little town?"

"No, I'm just here for the summer."

"And where do you live the rest of the year?"

"Los Angeles."

"Ah, City of Angels. I get there often."

She grew uneasy, but the man was spending hundreds of dollars. She could handle him for a few more minutes. "Where are you guys from?"

"Most of us live in Chicago. We're fraternity brothers."

"Nice that you've stayed friends." Patty glanced at Adam. Had he noticed Dennis flirting with her?

He was deep in conversation with one of the men, his tie loosened and glass of wine in hand.

Dennis leaned closer. "I'm in the wine country another few days. What would you say to…"

"Hey, Denny!" One of the men shouted with a drunken slur. He waved his phone in the air. "Just took your picture flirtin' with little miss red-head. Bet your wife's gonna love that."

The man lunged toward his friend. "Gimme that phone!"

The other guy jumped back. He knocked over a glass of red wine, stepped in the spill, and landed on his butt. The cell flew out of his hand and hit the floor.

Dennis ground his heel into the screen.

His friend on the floor let loose a string of obscenities.

Pandemonium ensued.

Tipsy barked, his tail wagging as if it were playtime.

Adam grabbed the wine bottles and moved them out of the way. "Hey, hey," he shouted. "This isn't a frat party!"

Patty, mortified by the melee breaking out, pushed herself into the fray and poked Dennis in the chest. "You're a jerk," she said. "And your total is eight-hundred and forty dollars. Gimme your credit card."

He handed it to her with a sheepish expression.

"And you, mister," she said to the one on the floor. "You made a mess in my shop, and I want it cleaned up."

The guy's mouth dropped open. "It wasn't my fault!"

"Quiet." Adam got behind the man and pulled him to his feet as if he were picking up a rag doll. "All of you need to settle your bills and get out of here. The police in this town are itching for some excitement, and I'd love to give it to 'em."

The guy looked over his shoulder at Adam. "You're full of…"

"Shut up." He gripped the guy's arm and pushed him into a chair.

Patty stomped to the register with the married jerk's platinum AMEX. How would she ever explain this to Tessa?

Dennis came back to the counter. "Sorry about that. I was just, you know."

"Yeah, I know, just having some fun. Well, look how that turned out." She pushed his bag toward him.

"You sure you don't want to catch up later?"

She tightened her lips and pointed to the door. "Get out."

The rest of the men paid for the wines they'd ordered and filed out like school boys.

The last one to leave, the only one sober enough to walk a straight line, apologized for his friends' behavior. "You can take the boy out of the frat," he said. "But, well, you know the rest."

"Yes I do." Patty handed the man his credit card.

"Can I, um, you know, pay for a cleaning service or something?"

Her anger diminished at his kind offer. However, the mess couldn't wait for a cleaning service. "Thank you, but no. Just make sure you and your buddies give Mariano's a good review on *Trip Advisor*."

"Absolutely. Five stars all the way."

"That'd be nice."

He left with an apologetic wave.

Patty closed the door behind him, turned the lock, and pulled down the shade.

36

With a sponge mop in one hand and orange-oil spray in the other, Adam was already cleaning up the mess.

"What're you doing?"

He spritzed the floor and slid the mop back and forth. "Mopping."

The night had been a big success, despite the skirmish, and Patty didn't want it end with friction. She watched his arms move the mop back and forth. "That was quite a scene, wasn't it?"

He pushed a hand through his hair. "I can't believe I'm finally making inroads with Tessa, and the first event I do ends in a fight. What'd you say to that guy, anyway?"

"Nothing," she said, taken aback by his tone. "Wait, you think it was *my* fault?"

"Uh, kinda."

"He came on to me, Adam. I did nothing to encourage it."

"That's not what it looked like."

Ah-ha. So he was watching.

"All I wanted to do was sell wine and make it a good night for Tessa." She put her hands on her hips. "And for you."

Adam rubbed the back of his neck. "Whatever."

"And just so you know, I wasn't flirting. Not at all. Why do married men like me? I mean, what is it about me that they think I'm just an easy…" Patty paused.

"It's the earrings."

"My earrings?" She touched the feathers.

He covered up his smile. "No. Some guys are just assholes, that's all." He went back to spritzing and mopping.

She sensed him softening. "Do you want to talk about last night?" She finally addressed the elephant in the room.

Adam leaned on the mop. "If you do."

"Well," Patty said, pressing the corner of her eye to head off the twitch. "I'm sorry I ran off. It's kinda what I do."

"Yeah, I've noticed that."

She chewed on the inside of her cheek. "I really liked the restaurant."

"It's a good restaurant." He propped the mop against the wall and put his hands in his pockets.

"And I had a really good time with—with you."

Adam inhaled and released his breath. "Hey, listen, I'm sorry, too."

"Don't be." She meant it. He'd only taken her on the best date of her life.

"You should know, Kamila was at my house to make amends." Adam sat. He rested his elbows on his knees and folded his hands. "Her parents are taking her to a new rehab place in Arizona. She has to start over."

Patty contemplated the notion of a fresh start. She recalled the pain in his ex's face as she begged Tessa to forgive her. For all the problems Patty had, none compared to Kamila's.

The sympathy she felt for a woman she hardly knew and didn't particularly like, surprised her.

"I did everything I could for her." Adam had a faraway look in his eyes. "But it was never enough."

Her heart twisted in sympathy.

His sadness was palpable. Whether he felt sorry for Kamila, for himself, or for the love he'd known and lost, Patty had no idea. All she knew was that she longed to put her arms around him, to comfort him, to be strong. A bud of confidence bloomed inside her chest. "Adam."

His head popped up, as if he'd forgotten she was there. "Yeah?"

Her moment to shine was upon her. She'd resolved to do better, to be stronger, and now was her chance to prove she could. Her lips parted, but no words came out.

He rose and came toward her, his gaze intense. He caressed her cheek, and his thumb brushed over the scrape. "Were you gonna say something?"

Patty nodded, but before she could speak, a loud knock startled her. "Don't move," she said, holding up one finger. She opened the door, assuming one of the men from the winetasting had returned for some reason.

It wasn't.

It was Liza.

"Sorry. I forgot my key." Her voice shook, and her face was streaked with tears.

"Liza, what's the matter?"

"Nothing. I'm fine. G'night." She practically ran from the room.

Patty leaned against the counter. She choked on a bitter laugh. "Never a dull moment, is there?"

"Nope." Adam picked up his dog. "Your sister's a lot of work."

"I guess." She wavered. A minute ago, he was going to kiss her, and she wanted that kiss more than any kiss ever. But Liza needed her. "I have to go see what's wrong. I'm—I'm sorry."

"Yeah." He wiped his lips with the back of hand. "You know, you might've been right."

"About what?"

His shoulders sagged. "About you being complicated."

"Oh." Patty walked backwards. "Yeah, maybe."

A complicated woman—the last thing Adam wanted.

She bumped into the swinging door. "Well, goodnight."

He smiled his crooked smile, but it didn't reach his eyes. "Take care, Patty."

She hoped those wouldn't be the last words Adam Hawk would ever say to her.

Patty climbed the stairs, using the railing to pull herself up the steps. Why did everything have to be so hard? And exhausting?

She opened the door. Liza was already in the shower.

Good. A soothing shower would give her sister a few minutes to calm down and put her *crisis-du-jour* in perspective.

And it gave Patty more time.

She ran down the steps, hoping she wasn't too late. At the swinging door, she halted at the sound of Adam talking to someone.

"I'll take care of it," he said.

She pushed the door open a crack.

He was standing by the window, his phone on his ear. "It's fine, Sophia, just let me know when."

Sophia? Why was he talking to his ex-future-mother-in-law?

Patty let the door close. She raced up the stairs and threw herself into the bean bag chair. If complications were money, she and Adam both would be millionaires.

Her brain flipped back to Liza who was still in the shower.

Patty needed a drink. Or chocolate. There was half a box of Milk Duds in her purse. She rolled off the bean bag chair and came face to face with Liza's open backpack.

Curiosity outweighed her good sense. Sitting cross-legged on the floor, she dumped out her sister's stuff—a pack of gum, a pink lip gloss, a set of measuring spoons, a small wallet, a letter.

A letter?

Patty turned over the envelope. She gasped. The handwriting on the front belonged to Maggie.

It was addressed to Liza in care of Nutmeg's. The envelope had been sliced open at the top, a bit of chocolate on the edges, as if a frosting spreader had been used as a letter opener.

Their father had always used a letter opener.

Her hands shook. Why had Maggie written to Liza? Nobody wrote letters anymore, not unless they had to. Not unless it was about something super important.

No wonder Liza was distraught. Their older sister was a master at causing distress.

She dangled the letter between two fingers and chewed the inside of her cheek. Reading the letter could have dire consequences.

If she discovered Liza's secret, she'd be forced to act. As long as she didn't know about it, she could pretend it didn't exist.

Ignorance is bliss.

Being kept in the dark had a definite upside.

The pipes clanged as the water went off. She stuffed everything back into the backpack, ripped off her clothes, and jumped into bed.

Liza came out of the bathroom and quietly moved about the room.

In the dim light, Patty stared at the wall and pretended to be asleep.

37

Harsh sunlight shot through the window, waking Patty.

She rolled over and opened her eyes.

Liza was sitting on the floor tying her shoes. In a minute, she'd be gone, and Patty could dodge the conversation again, preventing her sister's problem from becoming hers.

That is so spineless. Do better.

She sat up. "Hey."

"Oh, g'morning." Her sister flashed a tiny smile. She stood and pulled a Nutmeg's sweatshirt over her head. It looked adorable on her.

Patty's foot jiggled. "I didn't mean to fall asleep so fast last night. I, um, I know you were upset."

"That's okay."

"I'm kinda worried about you."

"Don't worry." Liza picked up her backpack. "It'll work out. Besides, there's nothing you can do. See you later."

Nothing she could do—what did that mean?

Before Patty could question her further, Liza was gone.

Nothing I can do about what?

It had to be about Maggie and whatever was in that letter. Patty chastised herself for not reading it when she'd had the chance.

But for now, the letter and Liza's problem would have to wait. There was a mess waiting for her downstairs and not much time to get it cleaned up.

Tessa might show up at any minute. Or not at all. Another unknown to add to her stress.

After a speedy shower, she dug through what was left of her clean clothes and found an old blue skirt she'd forgotten she owned. She threw it on with a tank top and sneakers and hurried down the stairs.

"Oh my God," she said, her hand on the swinging door.

The shop was immaculate. The wine glasses were hanging in the rack. The folding tables had been put away. The dark wood counters gleamed with polish.

Patty covered her mouth in disbelief. Adam must've stayed into the wee hours to get the place looking so good. She checked the floor, the walls, the shelves. Not a mark or a dent or a chip.

With no sign of the melee that had taken place and the shop in perfect order, Patty had time to track down Liza.

As if a motor had turned on inside her, she was struck with burst of energy and certainty. The time had come to demand answers from her sister.

Plus, she needed coffee. Patty dropped her phone into her skirt pocket and sprinted down the street.

At Nutmeg's, a long line of people snaked out the door onto the patio.

She got in line and checked her phone. Dead. She couldn't even remember the last time she'd charged it.

Patty tapped her feet, fidgeted with her hands, and made noises with her tongue. Finally, she got to the front of the line. "Oh, Trevor, am I glad to see you."

"Hey, Patty. Latte?"

"Yes, please." The aroma of fresh ground beans gave her a boost.

"Comin' right up."

She chewed on a hangnail, watched the clock on the wall, and tried to keep her anxiety in check. Confronting Liza would not be easy.

"Here you go." Trevor placed her latte on the bar. "I made it special just for…" He looked past her with a confused frown.

A hairy hand came from behind and placed a twenty on the counter.

"I got this," a low voice said.

The voice, the cologne, the arrogance…

Patty whirled around.

Dennis stood over her, a smug grin on his face. "Hi, there."

"I don't believe it. What're you doing?"

"Trying to be nice. Make up for last night."

"It's not necessary." She attempted to move past him, but he blocked her.

"Come on. I know you like me." Dennis smiled, showing off his bleached teeth.

"Actually, I don't." Something snapped, and Patty burst out laughing. "In fact, I can't stand you!"

Her shout attracted the attention of everyone there.

The married jerk backed up, palms facing forward. "Could you lower your voice?"

"Why should I?" Patty scanned the crowd. "Don't want people to notice you? Hey everybody, this is Dennis."

Half the room said, "Hi, Dennis."

She walked toward him. "Dennis is a jerk," she told the onlookers. "He started a fight at Mariano's last night. He thinks women can't resist him. And now it appears he's stalking me!"

His face turned red as a stoplight. "All right, I get it. I'm leaving."

"Oh, did I embarrass you?" she asked, every word wrapped in sarcasm. "I'm so sorry."

"Patty?" Liza emerged from the kitchen. "What're you yelling about? You're making a scene."

"I don't care!" Patty was drunk on adrenaline. She threw her arms open wide. "I. Don't. Care!"

She spun in a circle, releasing all the pent-up fervor that'd been building inside of her. It burst out of her like a champagne cork. "Hey, Dennis, where're you going? Home to your wife?"

Dennis backed away, his shoulders hunched, and tried to slip out the door, but she wasn't finished.

"And there he goes. The guilty husband. Bye-bye, Dennis. See you, never!" She continued her rant as Trevor came around the counter, picked her up, and carried her out.

38

Liza ushered Patty out of the bakery and back to Mariano's.

She closed the door and pulled down the shade. "Have you lost your mind? Who was that guy? You sounded crazy."

The adrenaline rush brought on by her outburst had worn off and been replaced by disgrace. It was only a matter of time before Patty's performance in Nutmeg's became the talk of the town.

"It doesn't matter who he is." Her eye twitched, and perspiration dripped down her shirt into her bra. "And I *am* crazy. Between Adam and Tessa and you, I'm losing my mind. You've got to tell me what's going on, Liza."

Her sister wrapped her arms around her waist. "I really don't think you want to know."

"You're right about that." Patty dragged her hands through her hair. "But I have to know. You said there's nothing I can do. Well, try me anyway. Start with Maggie's letter."

"How do you know about Maggie's letter?"

"I searched your backpack last night."

Liza tilted her head. “You had time to search my backpack, read my mail, and go to sleep before I got out of the shower?”

“It was a long shower. And I was only pretending to be asleep.” Patty found it remarkable how easy it was to be honest and transparent—no excuses, no justifications, no explanations. “But I didn’t read the letter.”

Her sister cocked her head. “Why not?”

“Because I thought as long as I don’t know what’s going on between you and Maggie, I could stay out of it. I didn’t want your problem to be my problem.” *Wow, this truth thing is liberating.* “And I still don’t.”

“Then why’re we talking about it?”

“Because I’m done avoiding it.” Patty clenched and unclenched her fists. “It’s more stressful to run and hide than it is to just turn and face the monsters.” She didn’t know where she’d found those words or the inspiration behind them, but it was true.

Liza gulped. “Wow. Okay. Are you sure?”

“I’m sure.” She braced herself.

Her sister opened her backpack. She took out the envelope and removed the letter. “I did something bad, or stupid maybe, and now…”

The bells jingled. Patty groaned. Would she ever be able to finish a conversation without being interrupted?

“Hi, girls,” Tessa said, shuffling through the doorway.

Nonna followed. She closed the door with care, as if not to wake a sleeping baby. She gave Patty hug. “Hello, dear.” She smelled like lavender, a walking pillar of aroma-therapy. “We’ve just been to the doctor. It’s not good.”

Thoughts ran around in Patty’s mind. It was barely nine in the morning, and Tessa had already been to the doctor? “What happened?”

Tessa removed her oversized sunglasses. “Evidently, my blood pressure’s bit high.”

“A bit?” Nonna said, unwrapping a tea bag. “You’re in

danger of having a stroke. I'm afraid we have some unfortunate news."

Patty's brain bounced like a ping-pong ball. "What is it?" she asked, fearful for Tessa's health and well-being.

The door flew open, *again,* and Cece ran in. "Patty, are you okay? I heard you had a total meltdown in Nutmeg's."

"I'm fine."

"I've been texting and calling non-stop. Did you lose your phone?"

Her brain bounced again. "I forgot to charge it."

Tessa lifted her head. "What happened at Nutmeg's?"

Cece put a hand on chest. "Oh, Tessa, you look—how are you feeling?"

"Crappy. Just tell me what happened at Nutmeg's."

Liza took over. "Patty tore into some guy. I've never seen her so mad."

"I'm sorry, Tessa, I just lost it. He was one of the men here at the winetasting last night, and, well, he was a complete jerk. But he spent a fortune. I should've controlled myself. I hope it doesn't reflect badly on the shop."

Tessa waved a hand. "It doesn't matter."

"It doesn't?"

"No." She sipped the tea her grandmother had placed in front of her.

Patty was stymied. "Why not?"

"Because there is no more shop."

"Oh stop," Nonna said. "That's not true. The doctor only wants you to…"

"Not work. Those were his exact words."

Tessa not work?

"Temporarily." Nonna looked at Patty. "My granddaughter is a workaholic who doesn't sleep and hasn't taken a day off in years. And the crisis with Kamila pushed her over the edge."

Patty's eyes burned. "I'm so sorry. This is all terrible and—

and shocking."

"It is," Tessa said, massaging her temples. "I feel like my whole world has fallen apart."

A feeling Patty understood all too well. "I've been there more than once."

Her mentor smiled sadly. "You certainly have, Patty, which is why I must apologize."

"To me?"

"Yes. I took advantage of your situation when I pushed you to stay in Clearwater. You were all set to go home and get your own problems figured out, but I made you change your plan. And what I said to you, well, it wasn't nice."

She recalled the conversation ten days ago and Tessa's exact words.

You live in reaction mode, responding to crises like a child playing hide and seek. You run and hide in a safe spot until it's not safe anymore, and then you run and find another safe place...

"But you were right."

"Yeah, I know. But I shouldn't have said it."

Nonna sighed. "I've tried for years to teach Tessa that not every truth ought to be spoken."

Cece blinked. "Wow, that's so perceptive."

"No, dear," Nonna said. "It's just common sense."

Patty pinched her forehead. All the truth-telling was giving her a headache. "It's okay, Tessa. You don't have to apologize for anything. But what's the plan now? What'll happen with your shop?"

"I don't know. My doctor wants to send me off to one of those relaxation retreats where they detox your body and some shrink makes you pour out all your mental anguish. It sounds like pure hell." She dropped her head into her hands. "I'm just so tired."

Patty held onto the back of a stool, trying to grasp Tessa's transformation. It unbalanced her. Everyone had roles to play in life, and they weren't supposed to change them. Tessa's role was to be in charge. She needed to be certain and controlling and authoritative, like Maggie.

Patty gasped at the parallel. "Oh, no, I forgot all about Maggie's letter. Liza, I'm sorry, you were…" She whipped around. "Where'd she go?"

"I think she might've gone upstairs," Cece said. "Want me to go check?"

"No. I'll call her." Patty pulled her phone from her pocket. "Oh shit, I forgot, it's dead."

"Calm down, I see her." Nonna pointed out the window. "She's talking to someone, a very attractive woman. My goodness, the woman looks exactly like her."

Patty ran to the window so fast she tripped and stumbled into the display, knocking over an arrangement of jams and chutneys and bread sticks. "Ouch!" She righted herself and stared outside.

Her two sisters stood beside a black town car parked at the curb.

"Is that Maggie?" Cece asked.

"It is." Her left eye went crazy. She grabbed her friend's arm. "Please tell me I'm having a nightmare."

"I'm afraid not." Cece squinted through the glass. "My God, they do look alike."

"Wow." Tessa put on her sunglasses. "Now I get it. You sandwiched between those two beauties? No wonder you're a mess."

"Tessa, that's another example of a truth that need not be spoken." Nonna shooed them away from the window.

Patty stepped back and waited for Hurricane Maggie to strike.

39

A few months ago, Patty would've run upstairs or out the back or into a closet. But she resisted the urge to slip away. Through the window, she could see Maggie's jaw moving a mile a minute, her finger pointing at Liza's distraught face.

Her older sister looked ready for lunch at the club—taupe linen dress, gold dangly earrings, and strappy tan sandals, a large designer tote on one shoulder. Her blonde hair was pulled back into tight bun at the nape of her neck.

People walking down the street lingered and listened.

Tessa tapped Patty's shoulder. "I think they should come inside."

"Right." She straightened her back, took a deep breath, and opened the door.

The jingling bells caught Maggie's attention. "Patty, hello."

"Would you mind coming inside?"

"Actually, this is between Liza and me."

Little hairs on the back of her neck stood up. "I think it's probably between all of us, so please come inside."

"We should," Liza said. "People are starting to stare."

If there was one thing Maggie couldn't abide, it was being the subject of gossip, even in a place where nobody knew her.

She pursed her lips. "Fine."

The three sisters filed into the shop, and Patty made introductions.

Maggie nodded in her usual refined manner. "Oh, Cece, you're Patty's friend from UCLA, aren't you?"

"I am. It's nice to meet you."

"Likewise." Maggie's southern accent, which came and went depending on her mood, was evident. She surveyed her surroundings. "This is a lovely shop."

Tessa stepped forward. She removed her sunglasses. "Thank you. I'm the owner."

Maggie offered a smile. "You must work very hard."

"I do. As does your sister. She's the best manager I've ever had."

"Patty?"

"Yes," Tessa said. "Patty."

A crease formed between Maggie's eyebrows. "Wait, you work here? Do you live here now?"

"No, but, well, it's a long story."

Her older sister knew nothing about the last two months of her life. And Patty preferred it stay that way.

Nonna rested a hand on Maggie's arm. "So, you're the oldest sibling, I can tell."

She blinked as if thrown off guard. "Yes. Oldest of five."

"I'm the oldest of seven," Nonna said. "To be honest, I found it very challenging. You know, curse of the firstborn and all that. Such responsibility, having to protect and manage the little ones."

Maggie tilted her head, and her eyes grew shiny. "You're so right."

"They don't call it a curse for no reason." Nonna took Maggie's hands into her own. "Now, I can see you have a purpose in being here, so we're going to excuse ourselves and let you and your sisters have some privacy."

"Wait," Tessa said. "I want to hear this."

"It's not your business, dear." Nonna nudged her out of her seat. "Come on, girls, off we go. I'll make us some tea in the cellar."

On her way out, Cece looked back at Patty. She raised her chin and gave a slight nod, sending a message.

You can do this. You're stronger than you know.

The swinging door closed, leaving the three Sullivan sisters alone.

Patty inhaled and let it out. "Maggie," she said, summoning all the confidence she could muster. "It's not that I'm not happy to see you, but why are you here?"

Maggie tucked a few stray hairs into her bun. "First of all, I know you're *not* happy to see me, but that doesn't matter. I'm here to pick up Liza and take her home. She knows that."

Patty turned to Liza. "You knew she was coming?"

Liza's blue eyes filled with tears. "I didn't really think she would."

So that's what was in the letter, *Come home or I'm coming to get you!*

"Unfortunately, I had no choice. Our little sister's on the verge of ruining her life."

"Come on." Patty rolled her eyes. "How does staying in Clearwater a few extra weeks ruin her life?"

Maggie's eyebrows shot up. "Is that what you think this about?"

Patty went cold. She pressed the corner of her eye. "Isn't it?"

"No." Her older sister took a deep breath. She had circles under her eyes and faint lines around her mouth. Her skin, usually bright and pink, was pallid. The last few months had taken its toll.

Patty's throat tightened. She knew almost nothing about

Maggie's life—what it meant to be the oldest and the only sibling who lived near their mom. Their father's death must have impacted her in ways Patty couldn't even imagine.

"Look," Maggie said, smoothing the front of her linen dress. "I'm exhausted. I just came to get Liza, take her home, and undo the mess she made."

"What mess?" Patty asked

Maggie put her tote bag on a stool. "Liza, do you want to tell her or shall I?"

"I will." Her bottom lip trembled.

Patty waited on tenterhooks for her sister to confess to something horrendous.

"I made a big mistake."

"All right." Patty said, recalling the bar incident with Rebecca. "Go on."

"A bad decision."

"Did you break the law?"

"No!"

"Are you pregnant?"

"Of course not."

"Geez, Liza, just tell me what you did."

"I quit school." She shrank like a tired tulip.

"What?" Patty wobbled. "You're kidding. Who quits Princeton?"

"The ones who don't belong there." Her voice was thin as a thread. "I only went because it meant so much to Mom."

Memories swirled in Patty's mind.

Princeton University, their mother's alma mater. She'd been devastated when Maggie didn't get in. A year later, she was furious when both boys were rejected.

Of course, Patty didn't even apply.

But when Liza, the golden child, got up to bat, she hit a homerun. And their mother was over-the-moon. The final Sullivan child had fulfilled the dream.

Suddenly, Patty was grateful for her big sister's presence and role as controller-in-chief. "What should we do?"

"Well, first, Liza needs to call Mother and apologize for the upheaval she caused."

Patty nodded in agreement. The authority in Maggie's voice brought her anxiety level down a notch.

"Okay." Liza sniffled and rubbed her nose. "I'll do that."

"Don't cry." Their older sister raised her chin with conviction. "There's still a bit of good news. Mother's old classmate works in the Dean's office, and she's expecting your call. You'll just explain how distraught you've been since Daddy died and that you withdrew from school due to—to a mental break brought on by overwhelming grief."

Patty let out the breath she'd been holding. Yes, that was all it would take. The perfect explanation for a rash decision

Liza would follow Maggie's instructions. She'd be readmitted, she'd return to Princeton in the fall, and the crisis would end.

Patty looked at her little sister, expecting to see relief on her face. But all she saw was heartbreak.

40

The revelation struck with more force than a bathtub falling through a ceiling.

Liza didn't have a mental break; she didn't quit school because their father died; and she didn't make a mistake. She'd made a choice. And in doing so, she broke her perfect record of being perfect.

Patty pressed her hands against the pain in her chest. Liza had been hinting at it for weeks. If only she'd tried harder, listened better, been stronger. Now it was too late.

"We'd better get moving." Maggie tapped her wrist.

Their little sister's shoulders slumped. Her blue eyes went dull. "Okay."

Patty's fingernails dug into the palms of her hands. Liza looked like a colored photo fading to black and white. "Hold on. I think we need to discuss this a little more."

A vein on the side of Maggie's neck pulsated. "There's nothing to discuss."

"Actually, there is." She took a tremulous breath. "Liza came to me because she needed my help. It took me a long time to realize what she needed, but now I know."

"You do?" Liza asked.

"I do."

"You don't," Maggie said. "Forgive me, but the only thing you know how to do is make a bad situation worse."

Patty accepted the insult. "I know I've done my share of making things worse. Lots of things. But not in this case. Maggie, you can't make Liza go home or back to Princeton or anywhere else for that matter."

"Of course I can, I have to. It's up to me to fix this."

"Why is it up to you?" Patty asked.

"Because it is. It always is!" Maggie's voice was biting. "And I'm the only one left. Daddy's dead; Mother's a wreck; the boys have gone back to their own lives. And you're hiding out here in the middle of nowhere. My God, Patty, for eleven years, you've acted like you're not even a member of our family. And now you think *you* know what Liza needs? I doubt it."

Patty felt the punch in her gut. Her sister was right.

Countless times she'd run away from her family, given in to fear and weakness. Her free-spirited persona was just a euphemism for what she really was—a screw-up, a shirker, an avoider of responsibility.

Maggie's skin flushed bright pink. "And besides, she never would've quit school if it hadn't been for you."

"What?" Patty swayed. "I had nothing to do with it."

"You kinda did," Liza whispered.

Patty wiped her sweaty hands on her skirt. "What're you saying?"

A sad smile spread over her sister's sweet face. "I came here to see you, Patty, to be with you before I went back to school. But you enlightened me. You showed me there's not just one road; we all have choices in life. And we need to do what we love. Or at least try to."

Maybe Liza *had* lost her mind.

Patty shook her head. "I never said anything like that."

"You didn't need to say it. You just did it. You came to Clearwater with no idea what to do or be, and you figured it out. You made a place for yourself." She sniffled, and her eyes glistened.

"I came here because a bathtub fell into my kitchen and I had nowhere else to go."

"But look what you found."

Heat rose through Patty's body. What did Liza see in her that she didn't see in herself?

"This is outrageous," Maggie said through clenched teeth. "Liza, go get your stuff. Patty, please, just step aside and let me handle this."

Patty licked her lips. Indecision made her dizzy. She had to be crazy to challenge the authority of the firstborn.

Maggie was competent and sensible. She brought stability to any situation. She took charge. She led. She governed. That was her role, assigned by birth order or IQ or personality. And Patty's role was to follow along or run away. She'd never questioned her role—and now was not the time to start.

Finally, after two months, nobody needed her. Cece's arm had healed. Tessa was closing the store. And Liza was heading back to Texas.

Patty could go home guilt free. She took a long, deep breath and waited for the calm that always came with the release of tension, the serenity she experienced whenever she ran away.

But it didn't come.

Her desire to run, to escape, to avoid confrontation leeched out of her in slow, agonizing drips.

"I'm sorry, Maggie," she said, her heart in her throat. "But no."

Her older sister looked at her as if she'd grown a tail. "No, what?"

"No, I won't step aside and let you handle it."

She narrowed her eyes. "But it's what you do."

"It's what I used to do." Confidence made her voice firm.

After spending two months with Liza, she knew what her sister wanted. What she needed. “Liza isn’t going with you. She’s coming with me.”

“I am?” Her sister’s eyes doubled in size.

Patty nodded. “If you want to.”

“Oh please,” Maggie said. “You can barely manage yourself, but that’s not even the point. Liza needs to go back to Princeton, finish her degree, and apply to medical school. She’s going to be a doctor. That’s the plan. That was always the plan.”

“Plans change.”

If there was one thing Patty knew for sure, it was just that. People died, bathtubs fell through ceilings, and little girls grew up and changed their minds.

She moved closer to Maggie. “I know this is your role. You take control, you manage and fix and oversee everything. And you make sure Mom’s okay. Aren’t you tired of carrying all that responsibility?”

“It doesn’t matter if I’m tired or not.” Tears filled her eyes. “It’s how it is, how it’s always been. We can’t change it now.”

Patty’s chest tightened. For the first time in her life, she felt sorry for her big sister. “Why not?”

The question hung in the air like a bird flying against the wind.

Maggie’s face contorted. “What am I supposed to tell Mom? I promised I’d bring Liza home and make sure she went back to school.”

Tears dribbled down Maggie’s cheeks, and her vulnerability opened Patty’s heart. After years of running and hiding, she was ready to meet her challenges and problems and fears head on.

“You don’t have to tell Mom anything, at least not by yourself. Liza and I will go back to Texas with you.”

41

Maggie studied Patty's face, as if seeing it under a bright light. "Are you serious?"

She nodded. "Yes. I have my own apologies to make."

"Well, I never thought I'd say these words, but I'm proud of you."

Patty met her big sister's direct gaze. "Wow. Thank you."

Liza spoke up. "Okay, so, what's the plan?" she asked.

Maggie ate a piece of cheese and looked at Patty with raised eyebrows.

"Oh, right," she said, off balance. Not deferring to her big sister was new; baby steps were in order. "Just to make sure we're on the same page, Liza—you want to stay with me, even though I have no idea what I'm doing?"

She nodded.

"And you're sure you don't want to be a doctor anymore?"

"I never did." Liza's eyes misted. "Even Daddy knew that."

"Really?" Maggie ate a cracker with cheese and fig jam.

"What'd he say?" Patty asked, hungry for any memory of her father's wisdom.

"He said it's my choice what road to travel in life. And if I ever discover I'm on the wrong road, I can always change directions. Can you believe how well he got me? I mean, *change directions*? It's exactly what I needed to hear, but I couldn't do. Not until now."

Patty shivered. The memory washed over her like a wave.

She was sixteen, at the height of rebellion, the Sullivan child who did everything wrong. "*Patty-cakes, I know it's hard to figure life out. And for some of us, it takes a long time. But you'll get there. You'll find your road one day. Just remember, it's never too late to change directions.*"

"Are you okay?" Liza asked.

"I think so." She glanced at the wine racks and the display of Hawk and Winters. Even Tessa had made changes.

An idea seized her and shook her like an earthquake. "Tessa!"

The swinging door flew open and almost knocked her down.

"Yes?"

"Were you standing there the whole time?"

"Only the last few minutes," Cece said. "I promise."

"I told them not to eavesdrop," Nonna said, bringing up the rear.

"It's okay." Patty cleared her throat. "Tessa, I have a proposal for you."

"What is it?" She finger combed her disheveled hair.

"I think—I think you should go to that retreat thing your doctor recommended and let me run the shop while you're gone."

Her mentor raised one eyebrow.

"And then, when you return, if you're happy with the job I've done, you'll hire me fulltime."

Cece hugged her. "You want to stay in Clearwater? Oh my God, that's been my birthday cake wish every year for the past three years."

"It has? That's so nice." She turned her attention back to Tessa. "So what do you think?"

"It's an intriguing offer, and I do appreciate it. But I, well, I don't think it's a good idea."

The wind in her sails died, and Patty's forward momentum halted. "You don't?"

Tessa put on her business face. "You've done an excellent job for me, truly you have. But running this place all on your own? I could barely do it, which is why I hired you in the first place. And I could be gone a month, maybe more."

"But, but, I thought…" Patty hesitated. "Are you saying you don't think I can do it?"

"It's not that. You just can't do it by yourself."

"I'll be here," Liza said. "I'll help her."

"I will, too," Cece said.

"Me, too," Nonna said.

"Me, three." Maggie put a hand on Patty's shoulder.

"You?" She eyeballed her big sister.

"Well, why not? I might come back for a week or two, you know, to visit my baby sisters."

Patty wept with gratitude. "You all want to help me? I can't believe it."

No matter what Tessa decided, it was gratifying to receive so much love and support.

The stressed-out, workaholic owner of Mariano's Cheese and Wine took a deep breath and looked at the ceiling. Her lips puffed out. "Give me a few minutes." She disappeared into the storeroom.

For ten minutes, nobody spoke.

The clocked ticked.

Patty watched the swinging door for any sign of movement.

Even Nonna tapped her fingers on the counter.

"What on earth is she doing in there?" Maggie asked.

"She's running the numbers, " Patty said. "Checking the

calendar for wine festivals, looking at how many tastings are booked, figuring out orders and deliveries. And if I had to guess, she's making a few calls."

A moment later, Tessa emerged. "Well, I ran the numbers and checked the calendar. There're a few festivals and tastings coming up. We do have orders to fill and deliveries to receive. And I made some calls. Keeping the shop open is a good idea."

She extended her hand. "Patty Sullivan, you've got yourself a deal."

~

The three sisters slept in the same room for the first time in over fifteen years. Patty gave Maggie the twin bed, and she slept with Liza on the blow-up mattress.

The following day, they flew to Dallas together.

Liza broke the news to their mother with her big sisters by her side. She wouldn't return to Princeton; she wouldn't apply to medical school. She would finish her degree eventually, most likely at one of the best culinary institutes in the country.

Their mother took the news better than expected. "You know," she said to her youngest child. "Your father told me time and again you didn't want to be a doctor."

"He did?" Liza's blue eyes widened.

"He did, but I pooh-poohed it. When you get an idea stuck in your head, it's hard to let it go."

The four women had finished dinner and were seated at their old places around the dining room table. The empty chair at the head stood out like a gaping hole.

"He's been gone five months, and I can't tell you how many times I've looked up to the sky and said, *You were right.*" She brushed away a tear. "Your father understood you girls far better than I ever could."

Patty sipped her mint tea. It was like an episode of *True Confessions*.

"You know what he said about you, Maggie?"

The oldest Sullivan child looked over the edge of her coffee cup. "What."

"He said you were afraid."

"Oh, please." She frowned. "What on earth would I be afraid of?"

"Of losing control, of being hurt, of letting others help for fear you won't be needed. But most of all, you're afraid that people don't like you."

A tear fell from the corner of her big sister's eye. "Well, well, they don't."

Poor Maggie. She was afraid. It was what Patty had seen in her two days ago. Nonna's words resonated—*curse of the firstborn.*

"And you, Patricia. You he understood best of all."

Patty sat up, expecting the corner of her eye to twitch. But it didn't at all, not even a little.

"Your father predicted you would search, struggle, and flounder for a long time before you figured out your life."

She bit into her upper lip. There had to be more.

"But he believed," her mother said, placing her hand on top of Patty's, "that when you did figure it out, you'd have the strength of a bull."

The strength of a bull?

She clutched her mother's hand in both of hers. A sense of calm spread throughout her body. Strength and determination filled her soul. "Thank you, Mom."

Her mother's smile was full of regret. "I should've told you long ago." She looked at the empty chair at the head of the table, the spot where her husband had sat for forty years. The formidable matriarch of the Sullivan family dropped her head into her hands and cried.

42

Patty and Liza stood across the street from the red-tagged duplex as a bulldozer plowed through it.

The sound of wood splintering, plaster cracking, and pipes breaking echoed through the neighborhood. But while the walls fell down and the roof caved in, Patty's chest expanded.

The last five months, filled with grief, shock, and revelations, had given her the kick in the butt she needed to change her life—to find the road she was meant to travel.

As the tracks rolled over the debris, Patty picked up Liza hand. "You ready to go?" she asked.

Her sister nodded. "Are you?"

"Absolutely."

~

Three days after the demolition, Patty's new job, and new life, officially began.

"Well, what do you think?" she asked Cece, smoothing the front of her bright white apron, a gift from Tessa.

It had *Mariano's Cheese and Wine* printed in burgundy script across the front. Embroidered in black thread in the upper left corner it said:

Patty Sullivan
Manager

Cece pointed to the word. "*Manager.* I love it."

"Me, too. I'm a little nervous. I hope I can handle it."

"I have no doubt you can." She picked up her dance bag. "Hey, you want to have dinner tonight? My last class ends at six."

"No, I'm doing inventory. Liza and Nonna are coming, and we'll be working late into the night. Needs to be done by the end of the week."

"Look at you," Cece said. "Being the boss—I love it."

Patty wiggled her shoulders. She loved it, too.

"Hey, don't forget family dinner on Sunday. Remind Liza she's in charge of dessert." Cece lifted her bag onto her shoulder. Her sapphire eyes shined. "Have I told you how happy I am you're here?"

"Not today."

Her friend laughed. "You're a funny girl, missy." She walked out, jingling the bells on the knob.

Patty tightened the bow on the back of her apron and rubbed her hands together. She'd pinched herself a dozen times—manager of one of the most successful gourmet shops in the region. Mindboggling.

All around she saw touches of herself—displays she'd arranged, new items she'd suggested, sample gift baskets she'd created.

Her father was right. She'd struggled for years, changed

directions a million times, fallen down, messed up, and made countless mistakes. But every misstep had been worth it.

Patty went outside. She opened her arms wide and tilted her face toward the cloudless sky. *Look at me, Dad. I've found my road.*

~

The first few days were a whirlwind, and she hardly came up for air. But whenever Patty stopped for a moment, her mind wandered back to Adam Hawk. He hadn't called her, and she couldn't bring herself to call him, not after the winetasting debacle and the way the night had ended. She cringed just thinking about it.

Her only hope was that their paths would cross. Until then, it was a stalemate.

After one week, Patty grew tired of waiting. If he wasn't going to make the first move, then she would.

It was a warm evening in late July when Patty decided what that move would be. She closed the shop and went to work on a special basket. Double cream brie, gourmet crackers, jalapeno plum jam, spiced nuts, and glazed apricots dipped in dark chocolate. She smiled at the selection—*sweet, savory, a bit of spice.*

In the middle of the delicacies she placed a bottle of her favorite Prosecco, covered the basket with a tea towel, and put on her red boots.

Armed with food, wine, and fabulous shoes, Patty went in search of her Greek god.

The huge, shimmering sun slipped beneath the horizon as she drove up the long driveway, parked in front the ranch house, and marched up the steps with basket in hand. The sound of her thumping heart echoed inside her head.

She knocked.

She knocked harder.

A dog barked in the distance. *Tipsy?*

Patty reversed course. Barely breathing, she walked down the steps and headed toward the vineyard, certain the little brown mutt would greet her.

As she rounded the corner of the house, an enormous Golden Retriever emerged from between the vines and bounded toward her. The dog was followed by a middle-aged man in rubber boots and red stained overalls.

The man let out a piercing whistle, and the dog halted.

"Can I help you?"

"I, um, I'm here to see Adam. Is he home?"

"He's not." The man wiped his hands on his legs. "Last I heard he was still in Arizona."

"Arizona?"

"Yep. I expect he'll be back soon though. We got grapes that need…"

She stopped listening. *Arizona—where Kamila was headed. Had he gone with her?*

Without warning, the retriever leapt up and knocked the basket out of her hands, sending it into the air. The gourmet items Patty had so carefully selected flew out. The sparkling wine hit the ground and burst open, spraying her red boots.

As if he'd known it was there, the dog grabbed the brie and took off.

His owner ran after him. "Bad boy! You bad dog, come back here!"

Patty looked down at her beautiful boots. The world was sending her a message, and she needed to receive it.

The stars were not aligning.

She and Adam were not meant to be.

~

Patty returned to the loft exhausted and deflated. Her grand plan to charm and impress Adam had failed, the lovely gift she'd made him ruined.

She got in the shower and let the hot water pound on her skin until it turned bright red. If water could wash away sadness, she'd stay in there all night.

Patty stepped onto the bathmat and wrapped herself in a towel. She wiped the condensation off the mirror with her hand and stared at the blurry face it reflected. "Buck up," she said to herself, "nobody likes a sore loser."

She dried her body and combed her overgrown hair. Maybe she'd chop it all off or dye it green. With so many changes in her life, a new hairdo sounded like a good idea.

In her Minnie Mouse nightshirt, a pair of cut-off shorts, and fuzzy slippers Patty went downstairs to finish some work. She opened her laptop and checked on a delivery of Zinfandel from a winery in Santa Rosa.

Her stomach growled. She looked at the clock on the wall. Eight-thirty, and she hadn't had dinner. She couldn't even remember if she'd eaten lunch. There was pizza place down the street, so she called in an order.

"Large mushroom and pepperoni," she said. "With extra cheese, please."

"You got it. Want it delivered?"

She looked down at her fuzzy slippers. "That'd be great."

"See you soon."

Patty ended the call and texted Liza.

Want pizza? (pizza emoji)

"Sure. Save me some. Still baking (cookie emoji)

. . .

(thumbs-up emoji)

She confirmed the delivery date for the Zinfandel, placed an order for a dozen gourmet salt sets, two cases of flavored olive oils, and a wheel of Challerhocker cheese from Switzerland. Then she clicked on a pop-up and fell into the rabbit hole of celebrity gossip sites.

A loud knock alerted her to the pizza's arrival.

Patty closed her laptop on the latest Bachelorette and opened the door.

A cute young man stood in front of her holding a large, flat box. "Hi," he said.

"Hi."

"You Patty?"

"Yep."

"Here's your pizza, large mushroom and pepperoni." He grinned and handed her the box.

"Thank you," she said, taking the pizza and giving him cash.

The delivery boy lingered. "You're Liza's sister, aren't you?"

Patty smiled inside. Her sister would be breaking hearts all over Clearwater in no time. "Yeah. You know her?"

He shifted from foot to foot. "Met her a few times." He glanced over Patty's shoulder into the shop. "She's not here by any chance, is she?"

"No. But you might find her at Nutmeg's."

"Right. Okay, cool." He backed up. "Enjoy your pizza."

The cute delivery guy jogged down the sidewalk in the direction of the bakery.

Patty closed the door, turned off the light, and carried her pizza upstairs.

She settled herself on her bed with the box in her lap and started eating. Pizza—the perfect comfort food. She was on her second piece when Liza walked in.

"Hey," Patty said, her mouth full. "You got here fast."

Her sister kicked off her sneakers and fell backwards onto the bed. "I'm so tired, and I'm starving."

"And I'm stuffed, so the rest is for you."

"Yum. Thanks."

"Oh, did you know there's a cute pizza delivery guy who's looking for you."

"Are you serious?" Liza lifted a piece of pizza from the box and started eating.

Patty laughed. "Totally serious. Do you like him?"

Her blue eyes danced. "Kinda. He's really sweet. We might hang out sometime."

"Well, that's nice." Patty scooted off the bed. "You want something to drink?"

"What've we got?"

She opened the mini-refrigerator. "Orange juice—half gone and expired. And one Diet Coke."

"Diet coke, then."

Patty popped open the can and handed it to her sister. She crawled back onto the bed, fell against her pillow, and groaned.

"What's wrong?"

"I hate to even tell you, it's so embarrassing."

"Tell me anyway. Maybe I can help."

"Well," she said, appreciating Liza's sweet concern. "I went in search of Adam today. I found out he went to Arizona."

Liza wiped her mouth with a napkin. "Oh, that's where his ex-girlfriend is, right?"

"I think so. Anyway, I'd made him…" Patty closed her eyes and put up her hands. "You know what? I'm letting it go. If he's back with Kamila, I get it." She recalled the pained look in his eyes when he talked about her going to Arizona to start over. "They have history, so maybe they belong together."

"Is that what you think? That they're getting back together?"

"I don't know." Patty let out a big puff of air. She pushed the pizza box to the foot of the bed and crossed her legs. "Let's forget about all that. I don't want to think Adam or Kamila or Arizona or anything. I want to hear about you and the cute pizza guy."

Liza's smile warmed Patty's heart.

They talked late into the night, as the stars appeared and a silvery crescent moon moved through the sky.

43

"Patty! Patty, wake up. I hear something."

She rolled over. Her head was heavy, and her eyes wouldn't open. "It's nothing, go back to sleep."

"No, really." Liza shook her shoulder. "Somebody's outside. Maybe the shop's getting robbed."

Patty looked at her phone. "Ugh, I forgot to charge again. What time is it?"

"One-thirty," Liza said. "Do you have a baseball bat or anything?"

"No, I don't have a..."

The window by the bed rattled, and they both jumped.

"What was that?" Liza grabbed Patty's arm.

"Maybe a bird."

"At night?"

Patty got out of bed. "I don't know. Do birds fly at night?"

"I think owls do," Liza said.

Whatever it was, it hit the window again and ricocheted off the glass.

Patty put on her shorts and slippers. She pulled an old

umbrella out of the back of the closet. "Come on, and bring your phone in case we have to call 911."

They tip-toed down the stairs like sneaky children. At the swinging door, Patty turned and faced Liza. "You stay here. If anything bad happens, run upstairs, lock the door, and call the police."

"I'm scared."

"It's okay. Probably just some stupid kids playing pranks."

Holding the umbrella out like a sword, Patty entered the shop. The glass refrigerator threw off an eerie blue light, and creepy shadows danced on the wall.

"See anything?" Liza asked in a hushed voice.

"Not yet." Patty moved past the counter and toward the door.

Something hit glass with a pop and then bounced on the ground.

With her heart racing, she raised the shade. A tall, shadowy figure stood beneath the window.

Patty opened the door and stepped outside with her umbrella in the air. "Hey!"

The figure turned. "Are you gonna stab me with that?"

She opened her mouth to scream then closed it. The umbrella clattered on the sidewalk. "What are you doing?"

Without answering her question, Adam pulled her into his arms and kissed her hard on the mouth. "You came back."

They sat on a bench in the park bathed in yellow moonlight. The air was fragrant with night-blooming flowers, and a warm breeze stirred the leaves in the tree above them.

"...so when I heard you were looking for me, I got in my truck and drove straight home." His hand brushed against hers. "I texted you from the road, but you didn't answer."

"I forgot to charge my phone," Patty said, still in a state of disbelief.

"I figured." Adam gave her a sidelong glance. "But I had to know for sure. Throwing rocks at your window in the middle of the night was my only option."

She laughed. "You could've come by in the morning."

"I couldn't wait."

He couldn't wait.

"After the winetasting debacle, I kinda checked out for a couple of days." Adam paused and rubbed the back of his neck. "The next thing I knew, you and Tessa were gone and Mariano's was closed. And nobody was talking. Anyway, I didn't know what'd happened, but I had to leave for Arizona. At least now it's starting to make sense."

Patty slid her moon charm back and forth along the chain. In the dim light, his gray-blue eyes looked dark and intense.

She took a deep breath. Being upfront with her sisters had liberated and enlightened her, and it had transformed their relationships. She could only hope it would work that way with Adam.

"I have something I need to tell you."

"Sounds serious," he said with the hint of a smile.

"Remember after the winetasting when Liza burst in all upset and I followed her upstairs?"

He nodded.

"Well, I came back down to see you. I thought we'd left some things unsaid." She twirled a strand of hair. "But then I heard you on the phone talking to Sophia. So I, um, I kind of freaked out."

Adam squeezed her knee. "Lemme guess, you ran back upstairs."

"Yeah. I did."

"That's your big confession?"

Patty crossed her arms over stomach. "That's only part of it."

He clasped his hands behind his head, leaned back, and stretched. "Tell me the rest."

"When I heard you were in Arizona, I—I figured you were with Kamila, you know, and that the two of you were probably getting…" She covered her face.

"That's not why I went to Arizona. It had nothing to do with her."

She uncovered her face. "It didn't?"

Adam shook his head. "I went to a winemaking conference in Scottsdale, and after that I went fishing for a few days with an old friend from school. To tell you the truth, I don't even know where Kamila is. And as far Sophia goes, we have some history. She calls me now and then."

The tension in Patty's body dissipated, and her shoulders relaxed. "I'm sorry I jumped to the wrong conclusion."

"Don't apologize." He rubbed the stubble on his face. "I'm glad you told me. In case you didn't already figure it out, honesty's important to me."

Patty pressed her hands to her chest. For the strong and silent type, he was being pretty talkative. And she hung on his every word.

"So, I'm gonna be honest with you." Adam rested his elbows on his knees.

She held her breath. For a moment, the air stood still, and the sounds of the night hushed.

"But before I say anything else, before I bare my soul, I need to know one thing."

"What's that?" The words almost stuck in her tight throat.

He turned and faced her. "I need to know if you're staying in Clearwater. Or at least thinking about staying, because I really want to give us a try."

"Oh." Patty blinked. "Well, yeah. I mean, I love my new job, and my best friend lives here." She touched his arm. "Plus, I kinda have a crush on someone."

"A crush? That alone is a good reason to stay."

"I think so, too."

"Okay then." He raked his fingers through his hair and sighed. "I'm kind of exhausted from the long drive, so I hope this comes out right." He searched her face. "I'm thirty-three, and I'm tired of dating women who bore me. You, Patty Sullivan, do not bore me. I know we haven't known each other long, but I'm falling for you. Falling hard."

She pressed her lips together. His words made her stomach flip-flop. A few hours ago, she was convinced he'd gone back to his old girlfriend. Now, he'd fallen for her.

"I'm falling for you, too."

"Yeah?"

She nodded and blinked back tears. Her Greek god was not beyond reach. "I have been since the day we met."

He kissed her with a gentle urgency that stole her breath and made her shiver. When his hand slipped under her shirt, trailing across her back and around her waist, Patty crawled into his lap. Her face hovered above his. He pulled her close and kissed her with parted lips, his tongue entwining with hers, his mouth hungry for every bit of her.

"Wait a sec." Patty sat back. She put her hands on his broad shoulders and felt his muscles contract. "You know, Tipsy had his eye on me long before you did."

"He's a highly intelligent dog." Adam stroked her lower back with his fingertips. "And he's never steered me wrong. Maybe I'll just run all this by him tomorrow. You know, make sure he approves."

She tilted her head. "You think he will?"

Adam's irresistible lopsided smile appeared. "I'm sure of it."

AFTERWORD

I hope you enjoyed Patty's story and your visit to Clearwater! If you have a moment, please post a review of *Road to Somewhere* on Amazon and recommend it to your friends. Reviews and word of mouth recommendations are the best ways to share your love of reading. Thank you!

Link to review Road to Somewhere

~

Come back to Clearwater and find out what happens next in...

Book Three
The Lonely Sommelier

Tessa returns from her stay in Wellness Camp rested and rejuvenated. But just as she takes two steps forward a surprise visit from her ex-husband sets her ten steps back. With some fun, quirky, intriguing new characters, you'll find

out how our controlling gourmet shop owner is faring and of course catch up with Patty and Adam.

Keep up to date and stay in touch by subscribing to my newsletter and joining my reader group on Facebook.

Links for E-readers:

Julie's Newsletter
Julie's Reader Group on FB
Julie's Website

ABOUT THE AUTHOR

Julie M. Brown is an author, playwright, and essayist. A California girl, she lives in Los Angeles on the Palos Verdes, California surrounded by trails, horses, random critters, and wild peacocks. Wife, mom, and dog-lover, Julie enjoys mentoring young writers and interacting with readers and bookclubs. When not writing, rescuing dogs, or trying out new recipes, Julie can be found in a quiet corner of her local library working on her next book.

View my website go to
juliemayersonbrown.com

And while you're on my website, be sure to subscribe to my newsletter ~ it's a great way to get in touch with me and to learn about my new books and projects.

Let's connect on social media, too!

ALSO BY JULIE MAYERSON BROWN

Long Dance Home

Book One in the Clearwater Series

A Clearwater Christmas

Young Adult Holiday Novella

Road to Somewhere

Book Two in the Clearwater Series

The Lonely Sommelier

Book Three in the Clearwater Series

The Amazing Eliza Landauer

Novelette

Made in the USA
Middletown, DE
11 September 2021

48020103R10158